BOSTON
PUBLIC
LIBRARY

Also by Doreen Tovey

CATS IN THE BELFRY
CATS IN MAY
DONKEY WORK
LIFE WITH GRANDMA
RAINING CATS AND DONKEYS
THE NEW BOY
DOUBLE TROUBLE

DOREEN TOVEY

Making The Horse Laugh

Illustrated by
MAURICE WILSON, R.I.

W · W · NORTON & COMPANY · INC·
New York

Copyright © 1974 by Doreen Tovey

ISBN 0 393 08703 4

PRINTED IN THE UNITED STATES OF AMERICA

1 2 3 4 5 6 7 8 9 0

MAKING THE HORSE LAUGH

Chapter One

Little did I think, when I was sitting on a horse called Rory going in circles in front of our local pub, that I would one day ride on round-up on a Canadian ranch. I was too busy wondering how long it would be before I fell off.

A vision passed before my eyes. Our little white-washed cottage in the valley, just round the corner and down the hill. Charles in the orchard inspecting his fruit trees, unconscious of my precarious plight. Two Siamese cats in the window, watching for me to come home. A donkey on the hillside leaning on her fence-wire in the hope that it might break. Myself, any minute now, being carried into the scene laid flat on one of the pub doors and what on earth I was doing on a horse. . . .

Actually it was Annabel's fault. Back in the days when we only had Siamese cats people never thought of our being interested in horses. But the moment we had a donkey—and there she was on view in the paddock, lending a distinctly racy air to the establishment—the local horse-owners all became friendly and this was the inevitable outcome.

It began with riders stopping to smile at Annabel while their mounts—big sixteen-handers most of them, this being hunting country—bent their heads over the fence and snuffled at her indulgently. It continued with talk of feed and fetlocks and how often did we have her shod? Not at all, as a matter of fact; she had a kick like a Kentucky mule. And it ended invariably with the question, did we do any riding?

"Not now," I would answer. "We haven't ridden in years. But one of these days we'll start again."

It was what we'd always intended. To live in country like ours and not ride is like living in Switzerland and not being interested in ski-ing. More horses pass the cottage any day than cats. Miss Wellington keeps a bucket and shovel at the ready at her garden gate. Father Adams, as he is always telling us, was barn and brought up with hosses—in token of which his legs have a decided Queen Anne turn to them and I swear get even more so when he's holding forth on horsy matters.

The one thing that stopped us riding was lack of time. There were the cats to see to and Annabel to exercise. The fruit trees eternally needed spraying or pruning or netting and you could never see our lettuces for weeds. Charles was making a new pair of gates for the drive. I had new sitting-room curtains on the stocks; the cats had been swinging on the others like cuckoo-clock pendulums for years. But work on the curtains went by the board when Rory appeared on the scene. Big, beautiful and black and mine, if I wanted him, for the riding.

He belonged to Mrs. Howell up at the Moat House. She'd bought him, after years of trudging up and down our hill leading her small daughter, Stella, on a succession of midget ponies, because Stella was now big enough to ride a proper horse and she thought it would be nice to have a horse herself and ride companionably beside her.

By this time, however, Stella was a very good rider indeed and while Mrs. Howell . . . wearing a riding hat with a somewhat desperate air as if it were some sort of talisman; crouched over her horse's neck even when he

was walking as if he was about to jump Becher's at any moment . . . while Mrs. Howell managed to keep up with her daughter, she certainly wasn't beside her. Rory, whom she'd purchased as a thin, lethargic, run-down animal who didn't need much exercise had emerged, after a month or two's rest and good feeding at the Moat House, as a high-spirited quarter Arab with a great desire to go. This not being on Mrs. Howell's agenda— nothing faster than a trot and stop if your foot came out of the stirrup was her idea of a horse—she rode everywhere for safety's sake behind Stella, in the manner of Sancho Panza.

"Don't look as if she be enjoyin' herself very much," observed Father Adams, eyeing her from beneath his trilby brim as the cavalcade passed our gate one morning. It didn't. It looked more as if she were longing for a parachute. Which made it all the more valiant of her when, with Stella away at boarding school, she undertook the exercising of both horses on her own.

She'd tried a couple of alternatives first. Persuading her husband to ride Rory while she rode Stella's horse, Troika, was one—but that hadn't worked, she explained to me later, because countryfolk being what they are, while it was all right for her to ride behind Stella, if Stephen perpetually rode behind *her* somebody'd soon start the rumour that they weren't on speaking terms. So they tried it side by side, but the moment the horses began to quicken pace Stephen had promptly got off —she'd got off too, she said; there didn't seem any sense in being foolhardy—they'd walked the horses home and that had been the end of that.

Next she asked a friend to help her out. The friend, who hadn't ridden since she was a child, which was a good few years before, borrowed some jodhpurs and came specially out from town a day or two later and I happened to be in the garden when the pair of them went past on their trial run. Mrs. Howell was over her horse's ears as usual. Her friend had the expression of somebody sitting on an anthill. Mrs. Howell was loudly telling her not to be nervous, she'd never fallen off Rory yet. . . .

That, of course, was because Stella had always controlled the pace. The moment those two got up on the open Downs—where, on a windy day, they should never have taken the horses anyway—Troika went into a gallop, Rory swept joyously up alongside him. . . . Mrs. Howell managed to stay on Troika but the next thing she knew Rory was flashing past her riderless, with reins and stirrups flying. When Troika eventually stopped—at the wall at the far end of the Downs, which was too high for him to jump—she found

Rory already there, looking smug because he'd won. Leaning down and grabbing his reins—she was terrified of doing it, she said, but she couldn't think of anything else—she'd turned Troika round, intending to trot back, leading Rory, to pick up her missing friend—and, with the Downs once more before them, the horses took off again.

It was like Gerard Hoffnung's story of the bucket. On the way back, with the horses going along the top

of the Downs like the clappers (Mrs. Howell had by this time let go of Rory and had her arms round Troika's neck) they met up with her friend coming in the opposite direction, frantically waving to try to stop them.

"Thee'st ought to have seen it," reported Fred Ferry, who happened to be up there picking mushrooms as he always seems to happen to be everywhere. "They went past she like a dose of salts and she sat down in the ditch. Thic Mrs. Howell had her eyes shut. Looked to I as if she were prayin'."

If she was, her prayers were unanswered. She didn't fall off and at the far end of the Downs, by the other boundary wall, she caught up with Rory again. This time, when she'd got hold of Rory's reins, Mrs. Howell got off Troika. She waited there, holding the pair of them, till her friend came panting up. They'd then walked shakenly home leading them and that had been that little essay over.

One must admit that she had courage. The horses had to be exercised, of course—but to continue trying to do it herself and to appear, as next she did, riding each of them in turn alone, certainly took some doing. True she kept them so tightly reined they would have done credit to a funeral procession. True she sat in the saddle positively stiff with apprehension. But she did it. And when, after some weeks of this, she still hadn't fallen off (not according to Fred Ferry, anyway, who was keeping a hopeful eye on her) and suggested one day that I might like to try out Rory . . . it would be marvellous if I would, she said, and he was quiet as a lamb on his own . . . if she could ride him, I could, I thought to myself. And without more ado I said "Yes."

So it was that next day saw me mounting him in the Moat House yard and walking him under the stable arch, down the curving drive, over the cobbled bridge and into the lane. It was all right as far as that. Mrs. Howell walked beside us talking and Rory could hear her voice. It was all right, to a degree, up the lane as far as the pub. Rory insisted on strolling while I wanted him to trot, but at least he went in the required direction. The trouble started when I tried to turn him down the lane by the Rose and Crown and, getting a sideways glance back along the way we'd come, he suddenly realised that we were on our own. No Mrs. Howell behind him on Troika. No Moat House dogs milling like a painting by Landseer at her heels. He stood there for a moment looking back across the fields at the house. Then, determinedly, he turned round.

Actually I didn't blame him. There he was living at the Moat House in the softest billets a horse could find. Another horse for company, people giving him pony nuts, Mrs. Howell, all Chanel No. 5, talking to him and fondling his ears. Made him feel really wanted, it did —and now I'd come along and was taking him away again. He was fed to the teeth with this business of being bought and sold. On strike he was. He wasn't going.

One mustn't give in to a horse, however. He has to realise who is master. As fast as he turned for home I turned him resolutely back again, which was why we were going in circles. What I couldn't do was to get him round the corner. I tried all right. I tried till I sweated. At one point a small girl came clip-clopping up the lane on a pony the size of Annabel, gave us a superior look and jogged nonchalantly around. Rotten little show-off, I thought, meanwhile smiling brightly at the audience in the Rose and Crown window and

once more urging Rory forward. At which he stood on his hind legs, walked backwards, and came down once again facing home.

I'd have been there yet if I hadn't eventually got off and walked him round the corner. I've described this before of course. How, once I'd got him round, I tried to re-mount in the road—only Rory was much taller than I was and I couldn't get my foot up to the stirrup. How I tried getting on him off a bank—whereat Rory got up on the bank too. How, outside Miss Wellington's cottage, I finally, with a superhuman heave, got on him . . . only to find, to his and my surprise, that I'd landed behind the saddle, on his rump. After which I hauled myself over the cantle, he started going in circles again and—being now back to square one—I got off, led him down to the cottage and shouted to Charles for help.

Charles is an indomitable horseman. One of those frustrating people who would still be glued to a horse's back even if it were turning somersaults. At my request he got on Rory and tried him out up and down the lane. "Safe as houses," he said, trotting him easily back and patting his neck. "Up on him, now. You can mount him off the gate. Take him up through the Forest—you'll soon get used to the feel of him and you can't come to harm up there."

All I can say is that some houses are safer than others and if Charles thought the Forest was foolproof, then after all our years together he still underestimates my potential.

I got on Rory eventually by standing on the dustbin. I tried it from the gate but found it impossible, with my feet back to front in the bars, to get my leg over a horse which, though Charles was holding its head, was doing a jig with its rear in the lane. I trotted off up the lane, too —by dint of Charles coming behind us so that Rory couldn't turn back. Then Charles dropped quietly away while Rory, the Moat House temporarily forgotten, high-stepped it up the track like a thoroughbred.

Till we reached the Forestry gate at the end, that is, and it was shut and I tried to open it. I only had to miss once as I leaned down and outwards towards the catch, and as far as Rory was concerned I'd had it. Couldn't open the gate for toffee, he snorted, backing away from it to make sure I couldn't. What did I want him to do, go over it? he enquired as I heeled him forward. Right then, now we could go home again, he said as, sweating slightly, I wheeled him aside. And he started at a spanking trot back down the lane towards the cottage.

Not that time we didn't. Firmly I turned him round,

made once more for the gate.... All this time the Hazells' small son Simon had been standing in their garden watching us. "Hullo," I'd called the first time I'd trotted past. "Who are you?" he called back suspiciously, not recognising me under my hat. "What are you doing on a horse?" he wanted to know when I told him who I was. I was beginning to wonder myself, but forbore to say so to a five-year old.

He witnessed the entire performance with concentrated interest. "Come back—I want to talk to you," he shouted as we retreated from the gate the first time. "Sorry, can't stop," I gasped as I went past like Paul Revere.

"You going to jump it?" he enquired as we came charging back at the gallop. "Not if I can help it," I muttered under my breath.

There is nothing more disconcerting than being watched by a little boy. I managed to stop Rory that time. I halted at the gate. I might even, had I been there alone, have eventually got hold of the gate latch. But with a pair of round blue eyes observing my every movement . . . the Hazells' garden abuts on the stream bank and he was now at the top end, right by the gate, watching me . . . I kept missing the latch by inches, got more and more embarrassed, and eventually, wishing I could sink through the earth, dismounted and opened it from the ground.

"You going to get on again?" enquired Simon as, having led Rory through the gate and nonchalantly shut it, I raised my foot equally nonchalantly towards the stirrup.

The answer to that, of course, was that I couldn't. I couldn't get my blasted foot up, any more than I'd been able to round the corner by the Rose and Crown. Casually, therefore, as if that had been my intention all along, I led him back through the gate, down the lane to a tumbledown piece of wall I'd noticed on the way up, got on it with the intention of using it as a mounting block. . . .

I'd just got my left foot into the stirrup when Rory took off. I didn't have a chance to get my other leg over his back. I was far too busy holding on.

"That isn't the right way to ride," came the parting observation from Simon, who—the Hazells' garden stretching a considerable length down that way as well—had run like mad along the bank of the stream and was still my closely critical observer.

That was what Charles said too when, having seen me off as he thought for a peaceful half-hour in the Forest, I came charging back in next to no time hanging on to Rory's side like a Plains Indian. What on earth would people *think*? he said. I'd have to be firmer with him than that.

Chapter Two

I was. I was so firm with that horse I developed arm muscles like a one-man tug-of-war team. But I never ever managed to get him round the corner by the Rose and Crown—I either had to get off and lead him or go a different way altogether—and I never, in all the time I rode him, ever returned to the Moat House on his back.

I never fell off either, mind you. But he had more ways of producing a situation where if I didn't get off voluntarily I would have done than one of Jane Austen's ingénues of inducing proposals of marriage. That first time, for instance, when I came careering down the lane along his side, Charles hoisted me up into the saddle again, told me to take him back to the Moat House by way of the valley bottom . . . no gates to worry about there, he said, and it would cut out going past the Rose and Crown. But I must make sure that I *walked* him and that he didn't get a chance to canter home.

The reason for this is that once a horse is on his way back to the stable, with the thought of food ahead of him and no more work for the day, he gets more and more single-minded. Let him get into a canter and practically nothing on earth will stop him; not even oncoming traffic or a tractor turning out of a field. I knew this well enough and not only had I no intention of letting Rory canter, for my money he wasn't even going to trot.

So I started out. Holding him so tightly at first that he positively minced, relaxing a little as I gained confidence and he showed no sign of bolting. Gosh, he was a super horse, I told him as we ambled along through the cow-parsley. We were going to have some wonderful times together, weren't we?

Not so far as he was concerned we weren't. At that exact moment he stopped dead in his tracks, said he'd seen a ghost and refused to go a step further. Under that bush it was, he said, pointing his ears accusingly at the far side of the track. Crumbs! There it was again! He leapt dramatically sideways into a patch of yard-high grass.

There was absolutely nothing where he was looking. No intimidating tin can. No fluttering piece of paper. No odd-shaped white stone such as Annabel delights in turning into a bogey. But I had to dismount to get him past the spot, leading him in a wide, precautionary circle through the grass. Then I couldn't get on again, of course—that was a foregone conclusion—so there was nothing for it but to walk back with him to the Moat House.

Many an equine tableau that house must have witnessed in the past. The old Squire riding out to hounds; clattering, pink-coated, on his tall black Irish mare over the cobbles under the old stone arch; open landaus with cockaded footmen bringing guests to Edwardian garden parties; the big horse-sledge with bells which the same Squire, eccentric that he was, used to drive like a Cossack round the snow-bound lanes in winter; the processions of ponies, with grooms and governesses and plump, straw-hatted children, that had marked the

passage of generations down through the years. What, I gather, it had never witnessed until the episode of Mrs. Howell and her friend from town, but was to see with considerable regularity during the weeks that followed, was a horse and its rider walking home, the horse having triumphed over the human.

Th'old Squire, said Father Adams, discussing the subject of my relationship with Rory at our garden gate one day, must be turnin' in his grave like a top. He'd seen people ride up that drive with collar bones broken, ribs broken, and their clothes all torn to pieces where they'd taken a toss out hunting. Many a time the Squire'd come home so roaring drunk, too, that when he got off his mare he'd fallen flat on the ground. "But they always came home in the saddle; they never walked," said Father Adams, stern disapproval in his voice. I gathered I wasn't half letting the side down.

I was sorry about that, but it seemed everything was against me. If we went back through the Valley bottom Rory unfailingly saw his ghost. If we went back via the Rose and Crown he got overcome with excitement as soon as he turned the corner and saw his home down across the fields—and, Father Adams notwithstanding about how they'd taught him to ride in the Yeomanry, riding a horse on his hind legs down a road with cars coming up it wasn't my idea of carefree exercise.

Sometimes I was grounded even before I got to the Rose and Crown. At the top of our hill lives a dog

called Bob—a big, be-ruffed white Samoyed who likes sitting and viewing passers-by through the bars of his garden gate. Originally we used to go past him with absolutely no trouble at all but one day it occurred to Rory to turn him into a ghost as well and after that, any time Bob was there Rory went up the bank on the opposite side of the road. Right to the top, and it's pretty high just there, so after sitting up there for a moment giving people surprises in their gardens I had to get off to get him down and once more he had me checkmated.

Partly, without doubt, it was due to my inexperience in handling him. Partly to the fact that things always happen to me. Charles could ride up the lane a dozen times and Bob wouldn't be at that gate, but with me—I could have taken a bet on it—Bob was always there. It was also a fact—it became more and more obvious—that Rory was playing a game with me. The object being to get me off his back, with no holds barred as to how he did it.

Never was this more clear than on the Saturday afternoon when I rode him once more up the Valley past the Hazells'. This time, I thought, I'd open that gate without dismounting if it took me an hour to do it ... but it so happened that the gate was open; we went through without a quiver. On we meandered, along the side of the stream, over paths yellow-carpeted with beech leaves which rustled crisply underfoot. I was just thinking that for the first time ever I looked like completing the circuit of the Forest, and wouldn't Charles be surprised when I rode back past the cottage through the other gate, when there was the sound of a shot up ahead.

We'd have to go back! He was scared of guns! said Rory, preparing immediately to retrace his steps. Oh no he wasn't, I said, kicking him in the flanks. He was jolly well going to go *on*.

He did. He went sideways like a crab. He rolled his eyes and snorted. But I got him past the old boy from the village who shoots pigeons in the Forest by permission. I got him past the old boy's light-coloured retriever, too, which was even more of an accomplishment.

We went on up to the ford, crossed it, climbed the

hill and were on our way back along the higher track through the pine trees when it happened. I was thinking that at last I'd got the measure of him. Rory had an air of sheepishness that you could see from the set of his ears. At that moment the gun fired again, way below us in the Valley—and Rory, catching me with the reins slack, took off like a pony express.

We were on a downhill slope and we were headed for home. Given those conditions there was nothing I could do that would stop him. We went down that winding red track as if we were on the Cresta Run.

A sea of pine trees swept upwards on the right of us. Pine trees cascaded steeply down to the Valley on our left. We wouldn't half take a tumble if Rory slipped over the edge—which, as I frantically tried to rein him, he showed every promise of doing.

I managed to slow him eventually, however, as we were going round a hairpin bend. At which point—he was still going pretty fast but I couldn't see myself braking him any further—I swung my legs over the saddle and slid off. Keeping a firm hold on the reins, of course, and expecting him to stop as soon as he felt my pull. Only Rory kept on going and I went down on my back.

Fortunately I still held on to the reins, fortunately I fell on the grass at the side of the track, and in that position I acted as a pretty solid anchor and Rory gave up trying to bolt. Why, at that point, should he want to? He'd once more gained his objective and got me out of the saddle. He stood there placidly eating dandelions as if I didn't exist.

Charles, I knew, would have insisted I got on him again. But we were still on a downhill gradient; he'd be off, I knew, the moment I got a foot in the stirrup and, so far as horses and I were concerned, discretion was the better part of valour. So, once more, we walked. Rory ambling along with the air of his mission accomplished, me keeping an eye open for a flat patch with a handy stone . . . it would look better, I realised, if I *occasionally* arrived home on his back.

No such luck. Rounding one of the bends I ran slap into Mrs. Howell on Troika. "Good Lord!" she said, turning pale at the sight of us. Used as she was to my walking up the Moat House drive, she obviously didn't expect to find me on foot out over the hills. "Has he thrown you?" "No," I reassured her. "I got off before he could."

At least, I hoped I'd reassured her. Troika being on the outward run and Rory hell-bent on going home, we didn't have much time for conversation. Just sort of hovered in passing, greeted each other and were gone. So I never did know whether it was Troika himself who got the move on, reasoning that if Rory was headed for home he'd better get back there fast himself or old Fatso would have eaten all the oats, or whether Mrs. Howell turned him at the top and came back to make sure that all was well. Hardly the latter, I would have thought. Troika was usually the one who decided when to turn. But no sooner had I got back to the Moat House with Rory and was unsaddling him in his stall than Mrs. Howell came clattering in.

"Thought I'd just have a short ride this time," she said, leading Troika into the adjoining stall. Troika snorted derisively; that was her story, we understood. "How's my boy then?" she asked, coming in to make sure that Rory was in one piece. As if by magic a chestnut topknot and an intimidating white eye appeared above the division between the stalls. As far as Troika was concerned she was his special human now. "Hooves off," he was silently warning Rory.

Something had to be done about Rory, though. That was obvious to anybody. He was getting more and more wilful, he needed firmer control than I could give him and I suggested that Charles should take him on. With his extra weight, I said, and the way he could handle a horse.... "What about those gates I'm supposed to be making?" asked Charles.

It was the gates or me, I said. I was getting dead scared to get on that horse but I couldn't say so to Mrs. Howell.

"Why on earth not?" asked Charles.

Because I couldn't, I said. I'd never live it down with Father Adams for one thing. And anyway, if he'd just take the wind out of Rory a bit I'd probably be all right.

So Charles put the gate-pieces on one side, dug his riding breeches out of the wardrobe and, to the intense interest of the cats who sniffed at them with exaggerated suspicion every time he came in, and to the chagrin of Annabel who protested whenever she saw him going up the path in them . . . he was going out on that Horse again, she bawled mournfully to the world in general; why didn't we Sell Her, then, if we didn't want a donkey any more? . . . he went off to deal with Rory.

For a while he did very well with him. He had no trouble getting him round the corner by the Rose and Crown. He had no difficulty when he wanted to open a gate. The sound of hooves cantering collectedly along the Forestry tracks, followed in due course by the appearance of Charles and Rory at the cottage gate looking as if they were ready for a dressage event at Olympia, made it look so simple that I was impelled to try him again myself.

I took him out once or twice after that. He certainly seemed greatly improved. Once I actually cantered him, making sure we were on an uphill run. Even that time I didn't reach home on his back, however. It was the one time when I might have done, but – I could have bet on that happening, too – way out on one of the Forestry tracks I met Solomon, our seal-point Siamese. He was about twelve then – it was some two years before he died – and I'd never known him so far from home before. It wasn't that he had followed us, either. He was already there ahead of us, sitting owlishly in the bracken at the side of the track as if he was intending to camp there for a week.

He jolly well wasn't, though. Not two miles out across the hills in the adder season. Whether Siamese intuition had led him up there – some unfathomable power of knowing that I'd be going that way coupled with the idea that that wouldn't half give me a fright . . . out there with that horse and finding him up there before me . . . I wouldn't know. Only that it is the sort of thing a Siamese mind is capable of; that I nearly had a fit when I saw him; and that, inexorably, off I got again. Walking home that time leading my horse with a Siamese slung over my shoulder.

It was the last time I was to feel even remotely safe on Rory. After that, though Charles was taking him out a lot, he began to play me up again. Something, I was sure, was wrong with him. He was becoming jumpier and jumpier.

Then Charles began to have trouble with him. One day he flatly refused to go the way Charles wanted him to and, when Charles insisted, Rory began to rear. Again and again, trying to get Charles out of the saddle, until – if he hadn't given in, said Charles, Rory obviously would have rolled – he was allowed to have his way and turn back.

He had become almost maniacally spooky about dogs, too. One day it was all Charles could do to get him past the end of a track up which, a few minutes before, a man had turned with a couple of terriers. He did get him past, but when half an hour later they came back that way again, Rory refused to go by in the other direction. So Charles rode him in circles, as I'd done outside the Rose and Crown. But with Charles it wasn't inexperience. This was a vital battle of wills.

Charles circled him, unable to get him forward, until Rory started to rear again. Only another rider happening along and deliberately crowding in on Rory got him past the disputed spot. "Damned horse wants a good thrashing," said the other rider. But Charles would never beat a horse.

What the end would have been we don't know. Whether it was Arab wilfulness, which patient schooling would have removed. Whether there was something wrong with him mentally – horses as well as humans can have breakdowns. Whether it was just that, having found a home he liked, he became more and more obsessed about not being parted from it....

The fact was, however, that it was now nearing Christmas, Stella was due home for the holidays, Rory was obviously unrideable—if not by her, certainly by Mrs. Howell. So Rory, who so much wanted to stay, went away again. Back to the dealer from whom he'd been bought. For a long time I never passed the Moat House field without thinking of the horse who used to graze there – black, superbly beautiful and confident that this was his home for ever. Now a sedate grey mare shared the field with Troika. Reliable, plodding – it wouldn't matter if she wasn't ridden for weeks.

That was the way it had to be, of course. Riding horses are for riding. But I hoped, wherever Rory had gone, he had a home he would love just as much.

Chapter Three

That is one of the reasons why we don't have our own horses. However unsuitable they proved – and there are few things more speculative than buying a horse – we would never be able to part with them. Once we took them on, if they bucked, bit or stood on their heads the moment we got on them, they'd still be ours for life. We'd worry about how they'd be treated if they did that to anyone else. We'd find excuses for them – perhaps they hadn't been treated well before. We'd get fond of a pair of dappled ears or the ripple of a chestnut mane, or be sorry because a horse turned out to be older than we'd thought... if we passed it on, what would happen in a few years' time?

Apart from that they are expensive to keep – even more so than Siamese cats. And they need constant grooming and exercise every day and a good big field to graze in. Ours is Valley land – rough-surfaced and very steep sloping. All right for a sure-footed donkey but not for slender-legged horses. Much better to hire them when we wanted them, we said. Or to ride friends' horses when they wanted a hand with them, as we'd done with Rory.

Only until Rory came along we hadn't got round to actually doing it. And after my experiences with him I realised how out of practice I was. So, when Rory had gone ... I'd made a beginning, I said, and now I was going to take up riding *properly*. Have lessons at the local riding school. Start again from scratch. Never again, I said ... already seeing myself astride a spirited steed in front of the Rose and Crown, a white one for choice, rearing high in the air with flowing mane and curvetting forefeet, while I controlled him effortlessly with the slightest pressure of my knees and the locals, looking out of the window, spilt their pints in admiration ... never again was a horse going to get the better of *me*.

Famous last words again. Five years later it is the avowed opinion of Mrs. Hutchings, co-owner, with her daughter Lynn, of the local stables, that when her horses see me coming they rub their hooves together in anticipation. I have an effect on them like nobody else she knows, she says. She has come to the conclusion that I have an electric bottom.

This is jumping ahead of myself, however. When, five years back, I decided to take riding lessons again local reaction varied considerably. Everybody knew about it, of course from the moment—doing my best to look as if I was merely calling about the jumble sale but my boots and jodhpurs gave me away—I was spotted by Fred Ferry going up the riding school drive.

He told the customers at the Rose and Crown – where, so I gather, the consensus of opinion was that 'tweren't afore time. On his way home Father Adams told Miss Wellington – who, having previously conveyed to Charles how nervous she was about my riding Rory, came trotting hotfoot down the hill for further representation. They jumped over *barrels* up there – she'd seen them, she told him worriedly – and we must think of the dear cats and Annabel. Supposing I fell off and hurt myself – who would keep everything going?

Charles, in fact, had already put an embargo on my jumping. Other than that it was all right, he said. I could certainly do with some practice. But it was easy enough to break an arm jumping – and at my age bones didn't knit so easily. Which might have been better put but he *was* thinking of my welfare. Unlike Father Adams, who apparently favoured an equine commando course.

Father Adams was our neighbour, mentor, factotum and, as the first person who'd made contact with us when we'd moved to the village, our oldest local friend. As such our achievements were his – to be discussed at the Rose and Crown as if it were he who'd written a book about the cats, he who'd painted one of Charles's pictures or he who'd taken the prize for dahlias at the local flower show – and so were our failures. His amour propre had been damaged considerably by my public failure with Rory and he saw my taking lessons as his one chance of recovering it.

If I fell off – that, I gathered, was all in the day's work. So they had in the Yeomanry, back in the First World War days when he'd been taught to ride. "No saddles – just a blanket and surcingle; no reins, arms folded," he said. "Two months and thee'st could either ride anything or thee wast back on thee two feet broom-pushin'." Country born, plumped on the backs of farm horses almost before he could walk and used to feeding and harnessing them when he'd worked as a yard-lad for the Squire, it hadn't taken him long to become proficient. Though, he said, it had seemed strange at first, riding a saddle horse himself like a gentleman.

He hadn't escaped all the broom-pushing, though. It seemed that as a potential Yeoman you were assigned a horse on entry, you fed him, groomed him, talked to him . . . if necessary, if he were ill, you even slept with him. And every morning at ten o'clock you paraded for stable inspection by the Colonel.

This was where the broom-pushing came in. You scoured your horse's stall till you could have eaten off the cobbles. Horses being unreliable, you then kept an eye on his rear. If anything happened you swept it up fast. "If nuthin' did," said Father Adams, warming to his reminiscences, "thee'st stood to attention by his head, kept one eye cocked backwards at his backside . . . thee'st could if thee'st had to," he said with finality when I queried the feasibility of this. And if, as the great man approached, the horse's tail lifted in warning and the ultimate calamity occurred – then, still at attention, you stamped two paces backwards, one to the right, and caught the jackpot before it hit the ground. "In what?" I enquired puzzledly. "In thee *'ands*," roared Father Adams, as if I could doubt what hands were for.

Thus burdened, you stood like a statue behind your horse till the C.O. was out of sight, then ran like mad for the manure heap. Woe betide you if you dropped any of it en route. For that, said Father Adams, you lost your walking-out pass that night.

Which is an interesting piece of English history and may well be how we won Waterloo, but it had nothing to do with my proposed lessons at the stables. I wasn't expecting to have to run for the manure heap up there. I did, when I got there, however, do riding without reins, and at other times without stirrups, with my arms very nervously folded. Round and round in circles on a sturdy fourteen-hander called Merlin. After two sessions of which Lynn Hutchings said I obviously hadn't lost my balance. What about some practice out on the open trail?

This was what I was after. Practice at going at speed. I'd decided, when I was on Rory, that I'd lost my nerve since I learned to ride as a child. Come to think of it I didn't remember going very fast even then. My grandmother, who'd been my guardian, had probably seen to that. No doubt informed the riding-school instructress that I hadn't a Mother (she always told everybody that) and... with her usual glorious inconsequence... that I mustn't be allowed to Fall Off.

I didn't remember cantering without stirrups either and when, way up on one of the Forestry tracks, Lynn said "Right now. Cross your stirrups over your saddle, we're going to canter," I nearly had a fit. "I'll fall off!" I said, conjuring up an immediate picture of Charles mincing up the cats' supper watched by two little orphaned Siamese. "No you won't," she assured me. "It'll help you to sit lower in the saddle." And so it did, and I loved it. It is one of the best ways of cantering ever – so long as your horse knows when to stop.

Merlin did. Merlin could have run a riding school on his own. Fourteen years old, he'd come to the stables originally when the Hutchings bought a companion of his called Gusto – a younger, brisker, more sturdy-looking pony which was the one that had really taken their eye. Gusto's owner, however, would only sell him to someone who'd take Merlin as well. They'd been together for six years now, she said; they must go together and she must have a guarantee that they'd never be parted.

Lynn had given it, had brought Merlin home more or less as a supernumerary, and had then discovered that, good as Gusto was, it was in Merlin that she had the bargain. Fourteen years sat lightly on his shaggy bay shoulders when he was out with the riding school posse. True, when he was on his way home again, up the steep old slaggers' path that led to the top end of the village, he would stop once or twice, droop his head and sigh. That was Merlin trying it on, said Lynn. Hoping his rider would feel sorry for him and get off and walk up. And on the next run out he'd be showing the whites of his eyes at the other horses and going as if he was on a race-course.

If, that was, he decided his rider was up to it. He knew people's capabilities better than they knew themselves. Put a beginner on him and he was like Nana in Peter Pan. Picking the safest path, slowing down if his rider lost balance, never attempting to race with any of the others. Once he knew his rider could be trusted, however, Merlin was up among the leaders. Going at a pace which, to someone who'd learned on him, was a considerable revelation.

It was to me, at any rate. There I was on one session, cantering confidently along on him without stirrups, Merlin lolloping as rhythmically as a roundabout horse and stopping automatically when we came to the end of the run – and a couple of weeks later he had me clinging to his saddle for dear life while he streaked across the Downs like a greyhound.

There were only two of us out on that occasion. Myself on Merlin and Lynn's assistant, Ginny, on Prince Igor. Iggy, a thoroughbred Russian horse, was a tremendous goer, Ginny was a first-class rider, and out on the open Downs she couldn't resist a gallop, never expecting me to follow. I didn't expect it myself, but there was nothing I could do about it. Merlin, his legs going like train pistons, just went. "Hang on to his saddle," yelled Ginny in alarm when, hurdling over some clumps of whortleberries, she looked back and saw me hurtling like Jorrocks behind her. She didn't need to tell me. I already *was*. "Well, he knows you're all right or he wouldn't have done it", she said when we eventually slowed down. "By gosh, he knows better than I do," I gasped. "I thought my end had come."

Merlin had passed me as safe, however, and so I moved on to Halberdier. Halberdier with the cart-horse feet and the Roman nose, who loved the hunting horn. . . .

To the onlooker one string of riding school horses looks much the same as another. Tall ones, short ones, plodding in line along a lane. "Bored to death and spiritless," somebody said to me once. "They can't have any character when they're ridden by so many people."

Anyone thinking that should meet Merlin. Or Gusto, whose mission in life is looking after himself. Mariner, now privately owned but who, when he was a member of the riding school, used to deliberately let the others out of their stalls. Halberdier with his massive dignity and his conviction that he was head of the stables. Or my beloved Mio, greatest character of them all.

I only rode Gusto a few times. One of my few personal experiences of his self-concern was when once, in the early days, I was out on him one icy winter's morning. True to his principles Gusto on that occasion was carefully in the middle of the remuda – keeping his nose warm in somebody else's tail with a horse on either side for insulation. Until, that was, we came to the ford on the way home. While the other horses splashed obediently through it Gusto waited till they had gone, walked determinedly, despite my efforts to stop him, along the bank – and, having found a suitable spot, jumped over. To everybody's surprise, including mine, I stayed on him. She should have warned me about that though, said Mrs. Hutchings. He wouldn't get his feet cold for anybody.

He had a robust appetite, hence his name, and like Mariner he was adept at opening latches. In his early days with the Hutchings he often used to let himself out of his own stall and into Merlin's at night, and the pair of them would be found side by side in the morning. On one occasion, however, Ginny put the horses' breakfasts up in buckets the night before to save herself time, laid them out ready in the stable corridor—and when morning came they found that Gusto had let himself out of his stall as usual but instead of joining Merlin had occupied himself in eating all the breakfasts. He was looking extremely innocent, with a "Who, me? Must have been some other horse" expression on his face. Only there was no other horse it could have been. On this occasion, for the first time ever, he hadn't opened Merlin's door. Deliberately, presumably, not wishing to share the spoils.

He was the one horse, said Mrs. Hutchings, that they wouldn't worry about even if there was an earthquake. When it subsided Gusto would undoubtedly be found in a meadow, by a stream, with a couple of haystacks handy for good measure, placidly awaiting better times and eating while he waited. Yet, she said, he was the kindest of horses. He took to all the small ponies, fussing over them as if he were their grandfather; in summer, when they were put out to graze on the hill, he was always to be found with the little ones, fondly keeping an eye on them.

He had endless ways of looking after himself. He could jump anything when he wanted to, for instance – when otherwise it meant putting his feet in an icy stream. But when it came to an actual jumping lesson ... when he didn't happen to feel like it or decided he'd had enough ... nobody had a better record than Gusto for stopping suddenly on the near side of the jump while his passenger went over his head. What was more, those who'd experienced it reported, not

only did one find oneself sitting on the ground still dumbfoundedly holding the reins – but on the end of them was an empty bridle, with all its straps still buckled. How he did it was known only to Gusto. Even an extra strap failed to keep the bridle on. It seemed – though nobody could be certain about it, however closely they watched him – that he'd perfected some extraordinary co-ordination of shooting forward his ears and opening his mouth, as his rider went over his head, so that the bridle met with no resistance and he slid out of it like Houdini. Whatever the secret, fortunately he didn't teach it to any of the others. One of them was enough, said Mrs. Hutchings.

I didn't experience that myself. I didn't – officially – jump. But there were still other unplumbed depths in that dear little pony's mind . . . or perhaps I should say unplumbed heights. I rode him one morning when I was wearing a mackintosh. Not a thing I liked doing – I always felt cluttered up in it. And when, coming down the drive from the stables, I felt a peculiar lurch under the saddle . . . it was my imagination, I thought. Gusto couldn't possibly have *bucked*. All the same I took the precaution of removing my mackintosh tails from his rump, where one usually drapes them to keep the saddle dry and the rain from running under one's bottom, and tucking them underneath me. If I should come off I preferred not to have my coat hooked round a saddle, with the consequent possibility of being dragged.

Up the lane we jogged in the beating rain, down the slaggers' path, up the trail through the pine trees to the stretch where we usually cantered.

"You've got your mackintosh under you – your saddle's getting wet!" somebody suddenly shouted from behind. "Oh – is it?" I said, making a show of spreading out my tails, allowing the speaker to pass me and then promptly tucking them back again. I wasn't taking any chances.

Which was just as well, because we had an exhilarating chase down round the horseshoe bend and up the other side – then, because the gate at the top was locked, back the way we had come . . . this put the observant one behind me again and once more, fortunately just as we got to a flat stretch, came the call, "You've got your mackintosh *under* you. Your saddle's getting wet." "★★★★!!!!" I thought darkly, hitching my tails out over Gusto's back. At which Gusto, worked up after his gallop, exploded like a Chinese cracker. There was no doubt this time as to whether he was bucking. In the middle of an admiring circle of six English horses and their riders, he put on an exhibition that would have done credit to a rodeo.

My hat was over my eyes, tipping further forward with every jolt. I'd lost both my stirrups, which were flying up and down like wings. "Belt him across his backside," yelled Mrs. H., tearing up from the rear where she'd been keeping guard on a near-beginner.

I couldn't. The only reason I was still on that horse was that I was hanging on to the saddle with both hands. Take one off to belt him and I'd be like one of those spiritualist pictures of ectoplasm . . . a line, which would be my other arm, still hopefully clutching the saddle, and the rest of me suspended above him in the air. Beside which, I'd seen Westerns in which riders belted bucking horses. The sequel was usually a cloud of dust disappearing hot-speed towards the horizon.

That, I somehow felt, I *wouldn't* survive. So I clung on like a leech, Mrs. Hutchings belted him instead, and Gusto stopped immediately and stood there like a lamb.

"I should have told you about that," said Mrs. H. "He doesn't like anything over his back."

Chapter Four

It was hardly to be wondered at that she hadn't thought to tell me. There were fourteen horses on the strength at the stables, any combination of which might be out together at one time, and to sort out who was likely to do what in any given circumstance . . . taking into consideration, too, who happened to be riding a particular horse . . . Complicated? said Mrs. Hutchings. It was like playing chess with the United Nations.

Gusto had this habit of bucking if his rider wore a mackintosh. Merlin, otherwise as steady as a sheet anchor, was apt to bolt if he had to go through brambles – they thought, from scars on his legs, that he'd been caught in barbed wire as a colt. Mio for some unfathomable reason was terrified of a fat little pony called Blackbird, who knew it and rolled his eyes at him if Mio tried to pass – which, since Mio was one of the fastest of the horses, meant that he must be put in front of Blackbird to start with or he'd be climbing up trees with frustration. Halberdier was as stolid as an elephant until he heard a hunting horn. Oh, and in the Spring, said Mrs. H. You had to watch him then. . . .

The Spring, it seemed, went to Halberdier's head. It went to all the horses' heads when they were first put out to grass. Out on to the hillside when they'd finished work in the evenings instead of sleeping, as in winter, in their stables. They rolled, ran races with each other, played hard to get when it came to coming in in the morning. Only Halberdier, however, felt impelled to roll when he was out on a ride. Which, said Mrs. Hutchings, you might have expected from a youngster but hardly from an eleven-year-old, 16.2 hands high and built like a Tudor battle horse.

They'd grown resigned to it now, though. The sun getting warmer daily, celandines starring the young green grass like the foreground of a Botticelli painting, apple blossom in all the gardens and a cuckoo calling from somewhere up in the elms.... These were the signals for Halberdier, plodding in sober riding-school file up the lane, to be suddenly overcome by the upsurge of it all, stop, kneel down and roll. Saddle and all, said Mrs. H. resignedly. They kept an old one specially for him in the Spring. One might as well try to stop a ship from sinking as stop Halberdier from going down. He was always the perfect gentleman, though, she said. He always waited, after kneeling down, for his rider to get off before he rolled.

Halberdier rolling and Mariner falling in love ... these were the signs of springtime at the stables just as Kelly's hayfever was symbolic of summer, autumn meant Halberdier again, this time wanting to go hunting, and winter saw the lot of them frolicking in the snow like puppies.

Mariner in love was really something. He was a gelding and couldn't do anything about it, which was probably just as well. Years ago Charles and I lived for a while in another part of Somerset, in a cottage that was opposite a farm, on the outskirts of a village. There was a high stone wall round the farmyard, but from our bedroom window we could see over the top.

Many an interesting scene that was hidden from the ordinary onlooker we witnessed from our vantage point. The farmer's wife, for instance, an erratic driver at the best of times, getting her car out of the barn after a tiff with her husband. Reversing full speed across the yard into the doors of the tractor shed and then, without so much as a backward glance though, she'd hit them like a battering ram, into bottom gear and out through the gate like an angry red bull on wheels.

The farmer himself, on another occasion, dispensing the traditional cider at the end of harvest. Hearty, masterful, clinking toasts with this man and that one, filling the mugs till they overflowed, from the big wooden barrel on the churn stand. And then, when the celebrations were over and the men had gone home, walking round and round the yard in desperate circles all by himself. Sobering himself up before he went indoors, not being quite the John Bull figure that the outside world imagined.

And, one moonlit night in summer, the most memorable sight of all. The farmer had a Shire mare – palest dapple grey with a mane like a spun-glass waterfall, and feathered hooves as big as buckets that came down like poundstaves when she walked. He exhibited her at shows, used her sometimes for ploughing or harrowing – sentimentally, for the sake of tradition, as other men keep vintage cars. It was a picture guaranteed to stop the passing traffic, he and Bess ploughing a red-earthed field together. . . . Bess, the majestic Amazon, in her glittering, brass-hung harness and the farmer proudly behind her, holding the handles of the great old-fashioned plough.

Normally she lived in the field behind the farmhouse where she could keep an eye on the family at mealtimes through the kitchen window, watch what went on in the yard over the gate and, when nothing else was doing, amble to the hedge which adjoined the road and put her head over it at passing children. What, then, the farmer was doing, suddenly bringing her in and leaving her tethered in the yard every night, we couldn't think... until we were awakened around two o'clock one morning by loud whinnying across in the yard... and... or were we imagining it... an answering whinny in the distance and the sound of hoofbeats on the road?

We were up in an instant, peering out of the window. Bess, plunging and protesting on the end of her long tether rope, looked like a charger from a fairytale in the moonlight – and even as we dithered, wondering whether the farm people had heard her or ought we to knock them up, down the road, his hooves sounding now like sledge-hammers, came another Shire horse. He was—it was hardly believable—the absolute image

of Bess. Galloping as if his future depended on it (it probably did; he was anxious to get there first) he came clattering powerfully down the middle of the road, silver mane flying, his great shoes striking sparks from the road surface—and then, beneath our window, he wheeled, gathered himself and jumped the five-barred gate into the yard.

It was a sight I have never forgotten. We were not very far at the time from South Cadbury. I have a fondness for history, particularly country history, and I was convinced, long before the archaeologists decided to dig there, that Cadbury Camp was the true site of Camelot. So much of the geography fits in, including many of the local place names and the fact that the Isle of Avalon to which Arthur, according to the legend, was ferried across a lake when he was dying, was the old name for Glastonbury—rising a few miles away from the flat Somerset peat moors that in Romano-British days are known to have been covered with water.

Whether Arthur's court was as glamorously romantic as Mallory describes it is another matter—but I was fascinated by Leland's account of a silver horseshoe that had been dug up, long ago, on Cadbury Hill... where would that have come from if not from some princely steed?... and the local legend that if one kept watch on Christmas Eve at midnight (and, some said, on Midsummer's Eve as well) one would see King Arthur and his knights, their lances flashing in the moonlight, riding down to water their horses at the spring at Sutton Montis.

Dead scared to go and watch myself, even with Charles for protection, I was intrigued to meet someone who had—a middle-aged no-nonsense spinster who said she'd gone up there with a friend one Midsummer Eve and they'd certainly seen something during their vigil

—though whether it had been the lances of Arthur's knights glittering or the eyes of some grazing cows, they'd never been really sure.

Be that as it may, it could have been Arthur's charger itself leaping that gate so nobly in the moonlight. And then the two horses met, and there was more whinnying and prancing in the shadows, and the sound of doorbolts rattling and a torch appeared in the yard. At which we went back to bed, satisfied that everything was under control and next morning would almost have sworn we had dreamt it—except that when we looked out of the window there were the two horses in the yard and a couple of strangers talking to the farmer.

They were another farmer and his son from some three miles away. Owners of the prizewinning Shire stallion that had jumped two five-barred gates and galloped three miles that night to mate with Bess, who, it appeared, was in season. And whether it was accidental or whether Bess's owner, in tying her in the yard, had hoped that he would, nobody ever knew. Only that it was a most fortuitous occurrence. And, to return to Mariner, that it was just as well he was a gelding because the way *he* kept falling in love, combined with his genius at opening doors, if he'd been left as a stallion there wouldn't have been a mare safe anywhere in the county.

A girl horse didn't have to be in season for Mariner to fall for her. At one time someone kept one in a field adjoining the stables. The other horses, said Mrs. H., took no notice at all but Mariner whinnied every time he passed her field, used to hurry back from the rides so that he could go and look at her over the hedge and, when he was jumping in the practice ring behind the stables, did it with his head turned firmly in his beloved's direction. So that he could get a better sight of her as he went over the jump—or was it to see whether she was watching him?

And when she *was* in season? I asked. Then they all went cuckoo, said Mrs. H. That was why they didn't have mares at the stables. They'd had one boarding there once—at livery, to use the proper term. When she came into season Mariner went off his food; the others, geldings or not, used to show off and fight and bite each other when they were waiting to go out on a ride . . . that was how Mariner came to knock her out, she said reminiscently.

"He *what*?" I said, eyeing the big, amiable-looking bay and wondering what could have come over him. Oh, he hadn't *meant* to do it, she hastily defended him. He'd really intended to kick Mio, who—no doubt deliberately, to annoy him—was standing between him and the mare. Only Mrs. H. had come up behind him to give him a final brush, he got her instead, and the next thing she remembered, she said, she was lying on the ground on the far side of the yard and thought there must have been an earthquake. And all the sympathy she got was that everybody said it was better for Mariner to kick her than Mio, she still had the bump on her shin and that had been months before.

When they weren't coping with Mariner's love affairs, then they had Kelly's hay fever. They'd tried just everything, said Mrs. Hutchings. Injections, inhalants, keeping him in his stable as much as possible when the pollen count was high. It was no use. Ten yards up the lane in hayfever time and Kelly was off. Sneezing, coughing, his black ears flat with woe, shuffling his feet along like an old man in broken-down carpet slippers, presumably so he wouldn't be caught off guard and fall down when he sneezed.

Up on the Downs it was a different matter. Whether the altitude cleared his head or he forgot himself at speed, he went like the wind up there, with just an odd sneeze or two as he galloped. Back again in the Valley, however, black Irish gloom descended. And stayed that way, so far as Kelly was concerned, until the rotten old summer was over.

After which, of course, hunting started and Halberdier resumed the stage. All the horses got worked up if they were out when the hunt was around. The huntsman's horn, the baying of hounds, the sound of other horses galloping—any of these was enough to set them off on an excited chase of their own. With, out in front, Halberdier, who'd once been an M.F.H.'s mount.

It was different in spring and summer. He was content then to stay in the rear all day if that was what was wanted. Lolloping along placidly with his outsize rocking-horse gait, bouncing his riders like pancakes on his broad-beamed carthorse back; it took someone the size of Henry the Eighth to sit down properly on Halberdier. Come October, however, with the brisk scents of autumn in the air, the bracken golden on the hillside and the frost crisping the short-cropped turf under his feet, and things took a different turn altogether.

The rule that one never passes the M.F.H.'s horse in the hunting field applied, according to Halberdier's interpretation, even when that horse was retired and working in a riding school, once it was the hunting season. A fact which nobody thought to tell me until I was out on him one day when I was incubating flu.

I ought not to have been there at all. My legs were like jelly. My voice was practically nil. I'd gone, thinking the ride would do me good, only to find that with every upfling of Halberdier's massive rump it felt as though my spine was being hammered up through the top of my head. He was out in front, too, something which I'd never known him to do before, thundering along in the middle of the track as if he were the lead horse at Agincourt.

There were six of us out that morning, including Ginny riding Prince Igor and holding a tiny pony called Snowball on a leading rein. Snowball, so small that he could only be ridden by children—which in term-time meant only at weekends—had to be exercised like this during the week; a fact which didn't worry him since without a rider he could, and did, get up speed like an express train. So, of course, could Iggy, particularly with Ginny on his back, and in next to no time there they were flying along in wide-stretched tandem with, like an immoveable tank, me and my flu on Halberdier, blocking the way ahead.

"Can you move over?" called Ginny. I tried to pull Halberdier to the right. It was like trying to alter the course of a galloping elephant. Halberdier stayed exactly where he was.

"Can you move *over*!" Ginny bellowed again. "Iggy's trying to get by and I've only one hand to hold him!"

I tugged at Halberdier's reins till my arms nearly fell off. Not only did it not make the slightest impression on him but, having lost my voice, I couldn't explain so to Ginny. She, thinking I hadn't heard her, kept yelling at me to get over; I kept pulling with flu-weakened arms at the reins; Halberdier, disregarding the pair of us, stayed firmly in the middle of the track . . . except when it looked as if Iggy and Snowball might get past, when he veered in a blocking movement.

When he did slow down at last I croaked my apologies to Ginny and she said perhaps it was just as well. If Iggy and Snowball had got by, in the mood they were in they might well have bolted. As it was she'd held them back and now she'd got them under control. . . .

It was also just as well, she said, that the hunt wasn't out that morning. In my frail state, if Halberdier had heard the horn, we'd have been in the next county by now. He'd done that once, she said . . . I hadn't heard the story? Of the time Halberdier joined the hunt?

Chapter Five

It had happened down on Exmoor. Twice a year, in spring and autumn, Lynn took a party there for a week. Horses and riders went by van and stayed at a farm near Cloutsham.

It wasn't the sort of trekking holiday where the horses do little more than amble, perched on awkwardly by teenagers in sandals and middle-aged Mums in slacks. These were fast, willing horses ridden by people who knew how, and the pace of the daily run was brisk. Down steep-sided coombes, through rock-bedded streams, up the narrow fox-paths on the other side and a gallop along the broad turf tracks on the top.

It was during one of these gallops that a lad called John, riding Halberdier, lost his hat and turned back to retrieve it. Having got off to pick it up, it had taken him a while to get on again, Halberdier being so tall and there being no handy hummock for mounting. He'd then cantered back along the hill-top, followed the track down towards a valley and, having reached a point where the path divided, was wondering which way to go when an old countryman appeared on the scene.

"There they be, up there!" said the old man, pointing towards the further hillside before John could say anything—and there, sure enough, streaming up towards the skyline was a group of riders.

John, telling the story later, said he'd wondered at the time how they'd got so far ahead, and why they seemed to be in such a hurry and nobody looking back for him. However he thanked the old man, touched his heels to Halberdier and was catching up to them fast when he realised his mistake. The horses and their riders were complete strangers to him. Somewhere ahead he could hear hounds baying. And then he heard the sound of a horn and realised he was with the hunt.

He tried to brake Halberdier, but it was too late. Halberdier had heard the horn too and was headed for what he regarded as his rightful place. Right through the lot he swept, fetching up ahead of the Master, with John, the colour of a beetroot, apologising wildly in all directions. "Grand old chap, isn't he?" said the Master when he'd heard the tale of Halberdier. "If he wants to come that much he'd better stay with us." So Halberdier spent the day showing them how to jump walls and ditches . . . ahead of everybody else, of course; he wasn't having any argument about that. And was he exhausted at the end of it? Not one whit he wasn't.

Lynn had taken her own new young horse, Jasper, along as a spare, and the next day she rode him, leaving Mariner free for John, so that Halberdier could stay behind and rest. The party was on its way up over Dunkerry when, hearing the sound of thudding hooves behind them, they looked back—and there, coming after them at a gallop, was a horse without a rider. At first they thought it was a runaway horse whose rider had come off—only to recognise, as it got nearer, the big feet and Roman nose. It was Halberdier. Furious at being left behind, he'd broken out of his field and chased after them. He stayed with them for the rest of the day, too, without a lead-rope or anyone on him. He bet they were going looking for that hunt again, he said. Did they think he was old or something?

And where were we while all this was going on? A thousand miles away on the Camargue. Looking at

bulls, flamingoes—and, by way of a busman's holiday, horses.

It was Charles's idea. I had suggested our going on the Exmoor holiday but Charles said he didn't like organised riding. Out on the range with the coyotes howling was his idea of a horse holiday, he said, never dreaming how prophetic he was being. Meanwhile what about a trip to the Camargue? They had some wonderful horses down there.

They certainly did. I had heard of the famous white horses, of course, and the equally famous black bulls, but it was like living a dream to actually see them ... not just a few in an enclosure for display but, as we drove down the narrow, pot-holed road across the marshes from Arles to Les Saintes Maries, in their dozens, everywhere we looked, like a constantly repeating background to a film. On this side a herd of bulls. Farther on a group of horses. Here, at the edge of one of the yellow-reeded etangs, a cluster of bulls and horses together. Over there, like a great pagan statue against the flaming Camargue sunset, a lone bull silhouetted on the endlessly flat horizon.

There have been horses on the Camargue for at least two thousand years, and the bulls have been there even longer. Some experts think the Camargue bulls are direct descendants of the primaeval bulls, others that they come from the wild ox. Whatever their history, there they are. Stocky, black, inscrutable. Dotted about the landscape like currants on a cake. Waiting for the Provençal bullfights.

This, of course, is why there are so many of them. In England one sees a herd of cows and maybe one accompanying bull. On the Camargue, the herds are all of bulls. And if, as I did, one feels a pang at the thought of what lies ahead of them—officially, at any rate, there is no cause for alarm. They are used for the Provençal type of bullfighting in which the bulls are never killed; may well emerge, garlanded with flowers, as the heroes of the contest; and are returned, after their performance, to their domain on the lonely Camargue marshes.

So we were assured, anyway, and were shown the mounted head, in the museum at Les Saintes Maries, of Vovo, one of the most famous of the Camargue bulls and the hero of many contests, who died peacefully on his owner's ranch at the ripe old age of fourteen.

He has a benign, almost smiling expression on his face and, according to the locals, positively enjoyed his appearances in the ring. Maybe experience gave him confidence. Personally I find it difficult to imagine any animal, brought from a quiet life in the wilds, being other than terrified by streets and shouting crowds and waving arms. But Provençal bullfighting—a direct derivation of the old Minoan cult of bull-dancing, introduced into the Rhône delta by the Cretans in the earliest days of Mediterranean trading—is as fundamental a part of Provençal tradition as is Morris dancing in England. And, from all appearances, much less likely to die out.

It consists of the bull—smaller and much faster than an English bull—being turned loose in a ring with a rosette between his horns. The ring is filled with the young men of the district, their object being to snatch the rosette with as much display of daring as possible, and whoever gets the rosette is awarded a money prize. The amount, announced over a loudspeaker, is raised

every few minutes. The longer the rosette remains unsnatched, the higher soars the prize. So, quite often, do the young men. The bulls wear leather guards on their horns to prevent them killing anyone but it doesn't stop them tossing, with the impetus of a pitchfork, anyone who gets in their way. Eventually, if a bull proves particularly difficult and the prize has risen very high, a second bull is let loose in the ring. This is the moment when an onlooker who is on the bull's side may begin to see some sign of balance in the contest. It is one thing for the young men to posture, rope-soled, arch-backed, bright-shirted, before the charge of a single bull, knowing that its horns are padded and if danger really threatens there are twenty or so other young men to distract the animal's attention. But when there are two bulls in the ring, it is a different matter altogether.

We saw one of these contests ourselves. The bulls were unharmed, each left the ring to applause—the top-flight Camargue bulls, we were told, make no more than seven appearances a year. Nevertheless there was only one moment I really enjoyed. I can see it now. The young man, red silk handkerchief held to the right of him like a torero's cape, backing seductively across the sand-covered ring while the audience suddenly went quiet. The bull, horns lowered, advancing with him, as if they were performing a paso-doble. The other young men standing still, permitting him his moment of solo glory as, long ago, did the teams of Cretan bull-dancers.

It was at that moment that the authorities let the second bull into the ring. He advanced quite docilely actually, standing in the entrance looking round him, undisturbed because for the moment there was a complete absence of noise. Then, over one of the nearby barriers, leapt a small white dog. Belonging to someone in the audience probably, and excited by the appearance of the bull. He didn't bark. The only sound in the pindrop silence was that of his feet, scampering across the sanded floor of the ring. Which the would-be torero, who had his back to all this and didn't know about the dog, took to be the second bull charging at him from behind—and without stopping to look he dropped his red silk handkerchief, streaked for the nearest barrier, cleared it as if he were jumping a volcano and fell flat on the other side. What made it so impressive was that he and the dog were the only moving figures in the whole dramatic tableau. The audience, and the bulls, all remained completely transfixed.

The bulls were the heroes of that occasion all right. They were cheered, garlanded, escorted triumphantly to the lorry that would take them back to the marshes, while the audience fought like a football scrum to pat them on their black satin sides. A curious mixture the Provençal, to whom a bull is an animal for baiting—and at the same time something akin to a god.

The bulls, and the Camargue horses, are raised on special ranches by wealthy men. Today these are generally industrialists, though traditionally they were Provençal noblemen. The most famous bull of all was Le Sanglier, The Boar—so called because he was particularly truculent and liked to be on his own. He died at the age of seventeen, having spent the last three years of his life cossetted like a retired racehorse in the courtyard of his owner's ranch. A monument was erected to him after his death and it is not only by humans that he is venerated. Even now, the locals will tell you, no bull will pass Le Sanglier's grave without bellowing mournfully in tribute—just as when the Marquis of Baroncelli, one of the most famous of all the bull-breeders, died in 1951, the bulls are said to have gathered on the marshes in groups to watch his funeral procession and bellowed in salute as he passed.

The Marquis also bred Camargue horses and was the owner of the legendary Lou Vibre. As far as these horses can be said to be bred by humans, that is—thriving, as they do, best in a semi-wild state. Their beauty, courage and endurance have fascinated men for centuries. Julius Caesar was one of the first to institute stud farms with the idea of supervising their breeding. Even Caesar was unsuccessful, however. Eventually, to keep them at their best, they had to be allowed to return to the freedom of the marshes.

They are small, perfectly proportioned and the true Camargue horse is always white. Their manes float about them like Rapunzel's hair and their tails are so long they sweep the ground. The ladies of the troubadours' courts must have ridden horses such as these— palfreys with silken bridles and tasselled headbands across their brows. Yet for all their fairytale beauty they are tremendously strong. They are never fed with oats. The salt of the marshes is said to be the secret of their astonishing stamina, just as it makes their hooves so hard they can be ridden without being shod. They rarely trot but, like the cow-ponies of the Western range, go straight from a walk into a gallop. They can cover thirty miles a day with ease and the Marquis de Baroncelli is said to have once ridden one of his horses, Sultan, from Les Saintes Maries to Lyons and back—a distance of 280 miles—in 43 hours. The Marquis lived for his bulls and his horses and when his favourite stallion, Lou Vibre, died, he was accorded the tribute paid only to the truly great Carmargue horses. He was buried, saddled and bridled, standing up.

So we were told in this place of legend, where the bulls are herded by gardiens carrying the symbolic trident of Atlantis; where ancient civilisations and their beliefs are but a veil's breadth away; where the vast salt marshes and the intense blue spread of the sky give one a feeling of solitude, boundlessness, and an almost tangible awareness of eternity that for me, at any rate, was never matched again until I stood on the North American prairies.

And that is a curious thing because the Camargue and the West are alike in so many ways. This business of the ranches, for instance. Much smaller on the Camargue, of course, and with salt marsh instead of rangeland—

but the ranch-houses look very much the same, and the style of fencing and the pole-built corrals. So too do the gardiens, the cowboys of the Camargue who herd the bulls, and their imitators who take out the parties from the dude ranches.

They wear the bright-coloured scarves, the high-heeled boots and the wide-brimmed hats of the American cowboy. When they are off duty they ride into Les Saintes Maries, tie their horses to a wooden hitching rail that could be straight out of Dodge City and troop off in groups for an hour or two on the town. The more I saw of them, rolling cigarettes as they rode, clattering down the main street in colourful cavalcade, the more I felt they must be copying the Western films—and never did it seem more like it than the afternoon I got caught up in a gunfight.

It was just after two o'clock. Les Saintes Maries, like most Provençal towns and villages, observes siesta from twelve to three and the narrow, sun-baked streets were deserted. There was only a long-haired tabby cat, tail raised like a potentate's palm fan, coming out of one turning and padding unhurriedly across the cobbles to another, and myself, en route for the baker's. Charles was waiting in the car in the square. We were going bird-watching on the marshes and wanted some pastries for tea. This little shop, bead-curtained and down a side street, was one of the few places that stayed open during siesta—the proprietress, no doubt with her eye on early retirement, not wishing to miss the chance of a sale.

I was about ten yards from the baker's when there was the sound of a shot. At first I thought it was a car backfiring—but then there were more shots, and then a whole fusillade, and out through the doorway of the bar at the end of the street tumbled a dozen or so crouching, gun-shooting cowboys.

The cat went up a side street like a rocket. I, less quick-witted, stood there open-mouthed, thinking alternately that this *couldn't* be real . . . I wasn't half a target for a ricochet if it was . . . should I dive through the bead-curtain of the baker's or would I look a fool if, after all, it were only a joke? Which, of course, it was. Even as Charles tore frantically round one corner to the rescue, a gendarme appeared blowing his whistle round another and the gun-fight dissolved into hilarious, back-slapping laughter.

The shots were blanks. The guns were toys. The cowboys, to amuse themselves, were enacting something they'd seen in a Wild West film. Westerns are very popular in the cinemas of provincial France and particularly so on the Camargue.

But when one works it out the gardiens, with their hitching posts, high-heeled riding boots and wide-brimmed hats against the sun, are not really copying the Western cowboys. It is the other way round. It was here, and from adjoining Spain, that this costume, this way of life, this preoccupation with horses and cattle and the traditions that go with them, went first to South America, then up to Texas and finally right through the American and Canadian West. The Camargue was one of the birthplaces of the cowboy—though only I could go there and get caught up in a pseudo-Wyoming gunfight.

Chapter Six

We didn't go to the Camargue just for the bulls and horses. Charles is keenly interested in birds, and the Rhône delta, offering much the same conditions as the land at the mouth of the Nile, is one of the few places in Europe where one may see storks, flamingoes and—though very rarely—ibis. It also contains beaver (the only place in Europe that does so) and wild boar. And while Charles wasn't too hopeful about the ibis and I didn't particularly wish to meet a boar . . . if we did, I had no doubt it would be when we were on foot and they'd have photographs of us in the papers, marooned up the nearest tree . . . we did want to see the beaver and the flamingoes—and, if we were lucky, an Egyptian vulture.

One might see them almost anywhere on the Camargue, of course, but the place where one could pretty well guarantee a sight of them—the birds, anyway, and the animals if one had sufficient patience—was the great 40,000-acre nature reserve around the Etang de Vaccares. Entrance to this is strictly controlled. In order to get entry permits we had to drive to Arles, spend a considerable time convincing an official of the Societé Nationale d'Acclimatation—who sat in his office in khaki shorts looking like Armand Denis, giving the impression that he's just come in off safari—that we were bona fide naturalists and not just bottle-top-strewing sightseers . . . and out we came clutching our passes. For two whole, wonder-filled days in the Reserve when goodness knew just what we might see.

We had it all planned. Up early in the morning. Presenting ourselves, food knapsacks packed, at one of the Reserve entrances as soon as we could after daybreak. No cars are allowed inside the Reserve of course; we'd be on foot for the rest of the day. Staying there right through till sunset. . . . Would two days be enough?

I regret to say that our visit to the famous Camargue Reserve lasted exactly ten minutes. We drove in through one of the gates, parked the car, presented our passes. . . . I wondered then why there were screens over the windows of the keeper's lodge and he certainly wasn't wearing shorts. . . . We started out, single file, across a wooden bridge, along a narrow track through shoulder-high reeds that skirted the edge of a rhine. Unseen creatures slithered and plopped into the water as we passed and I have never heard such a croaking of frogs in my life.

Neither have I heard the sound of so many mosquitoes. They descended on us like a swarm of locusts. The air was as black as thunder with them. The whine of their diving at us competed with the noise of the frogs. They covered Charles's back—he was leading the way in case of snakes or one of those boars—as if he were an outsize, irresistible fly-paper. I flapped at his back with a map and tried not to think about mine. At least I was wearing an anorak. Charles was in a short-sleeved shirt.

"It'll be better when we get out to that open space ahead of us," said Charles, quickening his explorer's pace considerably. "Away from the swamp and all this undergrowth."

It wasn't, of course. Out in the open the mosquitoes could see us that much better. They screamed in in their millions from every corner of the Camargue. Where ahead of us, a moment before, there had been a golden, Van Gogh-like landscape, now it was obscured by a positive fog, with reserves coming up at the double.

We turned and fled. Back across the bridge, into the car and slammed the doors. Some of the mosquitoes got in with us. We sat there and swatted every one. Then we held a conference. This, we decided, was a bad entrance to have chosen. We should have realised it was swampy from the map. No wonder there were mosquitoes here. The next gate would obviously be better.

We drove along to it. Three miles along a terrible, pot-holed road with Charles practically apoplectic at what was happening to the springs of the car. They left the surface like this to keep people away, I soothed him. He wouldn't like it if it were solid with tourists, would he? In the circumstances apparently he would. What was more, we discovered when we stopped at the next gate, it never would have been solid with tourists, filled-in potholes or not. Because, inevident though it was at first, here also it was solid with mosquitoes.

Boy, were they crafty. Not a sign of them as we reconnoitred cautiously out of the car windows. Not on the white, dusty, deserted road ahead of us, with the even whiter lighthouse in the distance. Not on either side of the car where it was white and dusty too, with clumps of isolated scrub on the hard-baked, salt-rimed soil. Not a twitch of one to be seen anywhere, even when we studied the landscape with binoculars. It *had* been that swamp and those reeds, we told each other. It was different here with this fresh sea-breeze, and if we kept away from the trees. . . .

I got out to knock at the gate, which was locked. The first one appeared the moment I opened the door. I stood and stared at the air, unable to believe my eyes. They were coming in like planes at Heathrow. In ones and twos at first . . . from their descent angle obviously from quite a distance. Then the air began to thicken. The crowd from the first gate had got the call-in.

Into the car, slam the door, wind up the windows. . . . Even then a couple slipped in with me. They splashed sinisterly red on the windscreen when I swatted them. Were there other poor devils, I wondered aloud, on foot on the Camargue?

It was probably his blood from the first gate, said Charles. His back felt all over bumps. It was too. It looked like a candlewick quilt and I was bitten all over my feet. I'd put socks inside my sandals—I'd heard there were *some* mosquitoes on the Camargue—and they'd pitched on them and savaged me, socks and all.

We gave up after that. This was in mid-September. Two weeks later, we were told, the mosquitoes would have gone. Or we should have come in May and they wouldn't as yet have arrived. Since we were there, I understand, the authorities have waged considerable war on the mosquitoes. There aren't nearly as many as there were and hardly a sign of them along the coast.

But for us, at that time, there was no going into the Reserve—we'd have been eaten alive if we had—and there was also no riding the Camargue horses. I'd promised myself I'd go on one of the treks that went out from the dude ranches. The horses, I'd read, could find their way across the bogs as if by radar, following centuries-old paths where no human could possibly go alone. True the trekking horses are now not always pure Camargue—they are importing Arab horses for riding and crossing them with the native stock. Needs must when the devil drives the barrel-organ, however, as Charles is always saying. The gardiens might look down on the dude horses—they themselves would never be seen on anything but a pure-bred white horse of the Camargue—but the others still looked pretty inviting, setting out in cavalcade into the marshes, and at least I'd have ridden along those paths. . . .

So I planned, before our experience at the Reserve. I rather wondered after that, however—and, watching carefully from a corral fence as a party set out the next afternoon, my suspicions were confirmed. A few yards out from civilisation and the riders began to fidget. Slapping necks, arms, faces, bare legs in shorts and culottes. . . . I winced as I watched them go. Literally sitting targets for the next two hours. Plodding irrevocably out into the marshes, where the mosquitoes waited for them like Apaches.

So we saw the beaver and the foxes in the Camargue Zoo instead and longed, hating cages, to set them free. We saw flamingoes at close quarters in the Zoo, too—and several times, in the late afternoon, we watched the wild ones flying. It was mosquito-free enough to walk on the shore paths beyond Les Saintes Maries, so long as one kept away from those scrub-like bushes. They zoomed out of those like guard bees from a hive, heading straight for one's ankles.

And from there we saw the flamingoes. Curving above the Reserve in a great vermilion cloud that rose,

swept gloriously westwards and then, banking sharply, flashed back across the sky like a scimitar—snow-white and rose-pink, now, with the flamingoes' backs to the setting sun. There can be anything from 1,000 to 1,500 in a flight, they say, and nowhere else in Europe can one see them. Once hunters used to shoot them but now, thanks to the Societé d'Acclamatation, they are safe.

At length, reluctantly in spite of the mosquitoes, we left the Camargue. Travelling along the coast to Le Lavandou where there were no flamingoes, no vultures, no beaver but, sitting on the almost deserted beach one day (it was now getting on towards October), we met up, in the way things seem to happen to us, with a most extraordinary turtle. About the size of a domestic tortoise, with a brilliant emerald green and orange shell, who came plodding straight towards us up the sand. We stared at him in amazement. We'd never heard of turtles round here. We looked for signs of a turtle invasion—but no, he was the only one.

Had he, we wondered, emigrated from Greece or maybe Africa, or was he a refugee from somebody's vivarium? Tortoises and turtles are inveterate escapers; we'd lost several ourselves in the past. He stopped in front of us for quite a while, staring at us fixedly. Was he resting after a perilous passage or hoping to be adopted? We almost did—but would they let him through the Customs? And how would our climate suit him? Even as we debated he got going once more, trudging sturdily on towards the sand-dunes behind us. We watched his colourful rear vanish valiantly over the crest. We'd have liked to have brought him back with us. But this, we thought, was more his natural environment—and he might have created havoc in Charles's fishpond.

So we came back to England—north from Le Lavandou, through a little town called Sollies Pont that made me think longingly of Solomon; through Beaune, Dijon, Rheims, congratulating ourselves on how the car was holding out . . . one never knows with an oldish car abroad and those potholes had been pretty excruciating. . . . The exhaust pipe fell off as we drove off the ferry at Dover, but that didn't matter. We were home.

Well almost, anyway. We had to collect the cats from Low Knap first. We tied the exhaust pipe on temporarily and drove back through the misty October morning, along the Sussex coast road, through the New Forest, into Dorset and then into Somerset.

It wasn't so bad to be back, remarked Charles. He wondered how his cob-nut trees were doing? I was looking forward to seeing the cats, I said. I wonder what they'd have thought if they'd seen those beaver?

Beaver indeed. They'd seen something better than that. Locked in their enclosure at Halstock as securely as in the Tower of London, *they'd* managed a confrontation with a mongoose.

It was a tame one, brought by Mrs. Francis from a pet

shop because she felt sorry for it, and short of being able to go back to India it now had everything a mongoose could wish for. Fresh meat to eat, a snug den to sleep in, an enclosure so large it hardly knew it was caged. It didn't like men—maybe one had once ill-treated it—but it would come to Mrs. Francis and let her stroke its head. It could have run free—they keep mongoose as house pets in India—but the Francises also had guinea pigs, which the mongoose might have mistaken for rats. And, said Dr. Francis, though it presented no danger to the cats, a mongoose running round loose would have created cross-eyed bedlam among the boarders. Just one of their own cats doing the rounds of the chalets was quite enough for that.

It had lived quietly at Low Knap for more than a year —hardly ever seen, mongoose being very shy animals. And why it decided to do a Colditz just when our two were there—its nearest neighbours as the crow flew— was beyond comprehension. But it did. Tunnelled under its enclosure wire, under a concrete path and an area of lawn, under another stretch of wire and the paved patio that surrounds each of the cat-houses—and came up in what in a film would have been the Commandant's Office. Beneath Solomon and Sheba's chalet floor, where it was trapped as securely as if it were in a cage. Knowing the mining propensities of Siamese cats the Francises had long since wired round the base of the chalets. And there it was found by Solomon, who proceeded to make the most of the occasion.

Not by yelling, which was reserved for being Up Trees and wanting to be rescued, Getting Lost and wanting to be found, or just exercising one's larynx— as at Low Knap—to see who was that week's champion for the Loudest Voice. But silently, as befitted a big game hunter. Ears pricked, neck stretched out like a giraffe, a look of intense concentration on his face.... Which combination caused the Francises, searching high and low for the missing mongoose, to wonder why on earth he was looking like that—and there, when they investigated, was the escaped one. Only too glad, after coming eye to eye with Solomon, to be rescued and put back in its den.

Apparently Sheba hadn't been the least bit interested. She'd seen millions of those, she said. Which was quite untrue but Sheba was like that—if it had been an elephant she wouldn't have turned a hair.

Solomon, however, was still talking about it when we arrived to take them home. Under There it was, he informed us, rushing for a last look under the chalet. Wasn't he Clever? he demanded as Dr. Francis picked him up. Didn't Want to go home, he howled as we closed the lid of his basket. Who'd they get to Stop It if it came up there again?

It never did. The Francises fixed its enclosure after that so that even the Sappers couldn't have got it out. He hadn't had such an interesting holiday in Years, bawled Solomon as we drove him and Sheba home. The same, though the memory of it was rapidly receding into the background as Solomon got up steam in the back, could be said of us and the Camargue.

Chapter Seven

That, however, had been the previous autumn. Now it was spring and I, perched like a mayfly on Halberdier's enormous back, was bounding manfully around our local hills. I was progressing, there was no doubt about that. I could touch my heels to him at the canter, which was quite a feat on him; the way he bounced his riders up, it meant doing it in mid-air. I could rise to the trot on him downhill, too, which was even more of an accomplishment. It wouldn't have been on an ordinary horse, but, as you rose in the stirrups on a downhill trot with Halberdier's great haunches jogging under you, you were pitched forward with increasing impetus till you nearly went over his head.

The first time I experienced it, I finished up round his neck. Ginny said she'd once cantered him downhill—she could canter anything anywhere—and before she knew what was happening she'd found herself holding on to him by his ears. It had been a pretty steep slope, she soon recovered herself—I'd never have managed such a feat. But I could now trot him downhill. I was very proud of that.

So there I was. Streets ahead of where I'd been with Rory. Encouraging nervous newcomers with tales of how easy it was, confidently performing the sort of mid-air Cossack dance with which one urged him on at the canter, nonchalantly saluting friends as I trotted through the village in convoy.... At which point Lynn put a spanner in the works by promoting me to Mio.

Father Adams had been wanting me to ride him for a long time. Halberdier's size hadn't fooled an expert like him. "Thee'st look like a pimple on a haystack on he," he said. "When be goin' to ride that Arab bay?"

Never, if I'd had anything to do with it. I'd heard too much about him. His speed; the way he ran off with people; his leap at the beginning of a canter that had left many a rider in the dust. It was like poetry to ride behind him and watch him go into action—those beautiful Arab hindquarters, gathering speed along the trail. But I preferred to read my poetry, not ride it. Imitating John Gilpin literally wasn't my idea of fun.

Nonsense, said Lynn when I expressed my qualms. Mio was wonderful to ride. He needed more controlling than the others—but I wanted to progress, didn't I?

Not right then I didn't. Not with that alert, dun-coloured head tossing up and down in front of me and Lynn holding the saddle for me to mount. A mettlesome white horse in front of the Rose and Crown indeed.... Why hadn't I settled for roller skates?

Pulling myself together, however... reminding myself that I was British, and that there is nothing about which one is expected to be more so than a horse... I climbed on. Mio didn't bolt immediately, as I fully expected. And with me in the rear the party set out.

Nothing happened on that ride. For one thing he only had to flick an ear and "Easy Mio," I said loudly, which ensured Lynn looking round to see what he was doing. For another, I kept him at the back. When we cantered, his gait was as smooth as the flight of a swallow

—with a barrage of horses' rears ahead of us, however, so that the swallow couldn't possibly swoop past. And the third reason, though I didn't realise it at the time, was that Lynn was with us on Jasper.

There were three really fast horses at the stables—Prince Igor, Jasper and Mio. Iggy and Mio very often raced each other, but neither of them could possibly beat Jasper. His father had been a racehorse, his legs were like long black stilts—even walking he far outpaced the others. So when he was out with a party Iggy and Mio behaved themselves, diligently conveying the impression that they Weren't Even Trying.

Not knowing this, I thought it was me. I *could* manage Mio! I told Charles excitedly when I got home. Gosh, he was wonderful! It was like sailing a dinghy with the wind behind you when he really got going! He hadn't leapt into the air when I started to canter, either. Those other riders must have been exaggerating!

It was several weeks before I discovered my mistake. Meanwhile I gained increasing confidence. I no longer kept him behind the others, for instance; I let him get up to the front. Why restrain a swallow when you know you can sit on his back? He never leapt into the air with me. Why should he, when I'd never had to curb him? When, as if glued to Jasper's jet black heels, he trotted and cantered and docilely stopped exactly when Jasper did?

The moment of truth came the morning Mrs. Hutchings took us out. No Jasper this time. Just an obviously experienced rider on Prince Igor, me on Mio, two or three others on the slower horses and Mrs. Hutchings perched loftily on Halberdier. She could and did ride everything from Iggy down, but she was never at ease on Jasper. He was too young and fast, she said, and to ride him in charge of the school . . . she'd rather leave that to Lynn, the expert, and be more firmly seated herself.

So there we were. Setting off up the lane, down the slaggers' path, across the stream at the bottom. Iggy and Mio leading, the others spread out behind. "Try not to let Mio race with Iggy when you canter," Mrs. Hutchings called from the rear. "If he does, he gets excited and that's when he gets out of control."

I wondered what she was talking about. Out of control? He was as docile as a lamb on a ribbon. I was still wondering . . . we were walking at the time, with plenty of time for rumination . . . when Iggy, slightly in front, quickened his pace just a little—and Mio took off as promptly as if he'd heard a starter's gun. What he'd registered in fact was Iggy quickening for the trot. The prelude, in a moment or two, to his going into a canter. Hold tight! We'd got to beat old Ig! said the set of Mio's ears. Couldn't have him licking us, could we?

We beat him by the simple process of not bothering to trot first ourselves but by shooting past him immediately at full gallop. I knew then what it must be like to drive a car whose brakes have failed. In my case I couldn't even switch off the engine. I tugged frantically at the reins. They might as well have been cotton threads. I grabbed at the saddle and shut my eyes.

He stopped at the end of the track. He always did, said Mrs. Hutchings when she caught up with us. It was his rider she worried about, not him. Once he found he could do it with a particular rider, too, he always tried it again. Next time I must remember to sit down hard and keep my hands down. It was the first few seconds that were important with Mio—to get him in hand before he got under way.

That was how I came to find out about his leap. It hadn't happened before because I'd never attempted to hold him. Jasper's presence had kept him in check on the previous rides and this first time with Iggy, he'd got away before I knew it.

"Right," said Mrs. Hutchings when we came to the next place where we could canter. Now sit down, keep your hands down—and hold him.

It sounds simple enough in theory, but not when your horse is on his hind legs, pawing the air with his front ones, and throwing his head from side to side to try to get free of the bit. "Sit *down!*" yelled Mrs. Hutchings. How, when he was perpendicular and I was practically horizontal? "Keep your *hands* down!" she shouted. Were they up? I was much too busy to notice.

They came down a moment later, though. I lost a stirrup and if I hadn't grabbed the saddle I'd have been off. This took such check as I'd had off Mio and, with the leap I'd heard so much about, he was away like a greyhound up the track. If I hadn't been holding the saddle I'd have come off then, too. He curved through the air like a dolphin. But I stayed on him, though very one-sided, and we went up the path like a rocket. Even faster than the first time, because Iggy was farther ahead. We passed him. We were neck and neck for a while. But we'd apparently grown wings and we did it. "Sit back and rein him *alternately*," Iggy's rider shouted after us. Was she joking? I dared not let go of the saddle!

If he doesn't stop at the end of the track, I thought . . . but he did, as he'd done before. We had to wait here for the others, he snorted. Gosh, but he felt good for that gallop!

This was it. It wasn't that he was a bad horse. Not even a temperamental one, as poor Rory had been. He was a three-quarter thoroughbred whose joy it was to go, particularly if he could have a race with Iggy. He needed an incompetent rider for that, of course—and boy! in me he'd found one!

"You stayed on him though. The rest will come in time. It's only a matter of practice," encouraged Mrs. Hutchings. Mio at that moment was busily eating grass. Did I imagine it, or did he twitch his ears? And was that, in a grazing horse, the equivalent of a wink? It must have been, because the next time out he took me steeplechasing.

I know what gave him that idea, too. He'd been cantering along . . . me still hopelessly out of control but at least I knew now that he'd stop. And then—"Watch out for this boggy bit—he always jumps this. Mind he doesn't shake you off," warned Mrs. Hutchings. He jumped it all right. He didn't unseat me because his jump, unchecked, was as smooth as touching down on velvet—and because, in anticipation, I'd once more grabbed his saddle and was clinging to it like a leech. His ears twitched that time. Definitely. As soon as we hit the ground. "She's scared of jumping . . . must remember that . . ." You could almost hear him saying it.

He got his chance sooner than I expected. We were ambling homewards, all well pleased with ourselves, Mrs. Hutchings discoursing on jumping. "You ought to have some jumping lessons," she said. "They help tremendously to give you balance." I couldn't risk falling off, I demurred. What with Charles and the cottage and the cats. . . .

Within seconds of saying that we rounded a corner and came upon a stretch where the Forestry workers had been felling trees. They were laid across the path at intervals, waiting for the tractor to come and pick them up. It was, admittedly, a track up which we very often cantered, but not when there were obstacles in the way. The others, led by Iggy, began to pick their way around the branches; Merlin jittery as usual in case his legs got trapped.

No so Mio. Want to see what he could do with this lot? he enquired, heading straight up the middle of the track. And before I knew it we were jumping them like Harvey Smith, right from the bottom to the top.

It wasn't nearly so bad as I'd imagined. After the first couple of jumps I actually enjoyed it. I'd grabbed for the saddle as usual, of course, but you couldn't tell that from a distance. Which was how a couple of Forestry workers, who happened to be in among the standing trees only I was too busy to notice them, arrived at the Rose and Crown at lunchtime with news that shook the regulars rigid. That they'd seen me hoss-jumping as if I was a blooming kangaroo and they'd never have believed that I could do it.

Neither would I. Even clutching the saddle it was quite a feat. He'd never done that before, said Mrs. Hutchings. He didn't even particularly *like* jumping. It was a silly thing to say, she commented, slightly puzzled—but I seemed to have an effect on him.

I did indeed. Not all the time of course. There were rides when butter wouldn't have melted in his mouth and it was the others who misbehaved. Blackbird nipping Kelly on the bottom, for instance, and Kelly—hay fever permitting—threatening to kick his teeth in. Merlin acting silly about a bramble patch, or Gusto doing a bit of bucking. And Mio regarding them, ears pointed forward, as if he'd never done anything wrong in his life. Weren't they terrible? said his attitude. You could tell *they* hadn't any breeding.

And I would go home and recount all this to Charles and tell him how proficient I was becoming, and next time out Mio would get the devil in him and I'd be right back where I started. . . . As, for instance, the day we went on to the Downs.

Up till now I'd only ridden Mio in the Forest, where there might be stretches he could take off on but at least, with the avenues of pine trees on either side, he couldn't go off the track. In the Forest, too, which was most important, the trees gave shelter from the wind, which acts on horses, particularly thoroughbreds, as if someone has stuck a pin in them. I knew this and, going through the gate, with the vast sweep of the Downs ahead of us, I remembered Mrs. Howell with Troika and Rory and prepared to meet my end.

It wasn't too bad at first. We headed downhill initially, in the direction of the old Celtic camp. *Walking*, said Mrs. Hutchings firmly—and, being unexcited, Mio walked, his feet cutting crisply into the short moorland turf.

"Now you can go," she said when we'd got down to the flat. "But be careful of his getting up speed when you reach the sloping bit by the clump of trees . . . and watch out for the potholes. Don't let him put a foot in those."

My heart sank to the soles of my jodhpur boots. Something else to worry about now. How did I see a pothole before I got to it? And how would I steer around it if I did? Remembering about being British, however, I said "Right ho" as nonchalantly as I could, resignedly gripped the saddle and off we sped, Mio and I, along the ancient hill-top track towards the camp.

Wide enough for a chariot it was, and with good reason. The Celts had a fortress up there at one time, and after them the Romans and later on the Danes. The horses that must have passed that way through the centuries . . . pulling chariots or baggage carts or galloping urgently with messengers on their backs . . . along that high ridge track with the sky all around it and the wind blowing in from the Severn. . . . And none could have sped more eagerly than Mio, as if every horse that had ever galloped it was somehow galloping with him. And I—I was his fearless rider, racing along the track to the fort. Down the slope Mrs. Hutchings had warned about . . . how many had noted its downward slant before me? On, as if our lives depended on it, towards the distant, tumbled ramparts of the fort.

For the moment I really was fearless, there was such exhilaration about our going. I spotted a pothole . . . I steered him round it . . . I actually *could* do it. . . . And he was bound to stop, I reasoned, when we got to the camp.

He did. He halted, his sides heaving, where the track ran through the grassy mounds that had once been the gateway. We looked back. The others were still coming in the distance, as in another world. I patted his sleek dun neck. He and I were as one. Together we could do anything.

So long, that is, as it was of Mio's choosing. Once

the others had come up with us we turned and went back the same way. A *gentle* canter this time, said Mrs. Hutchings. The horses had done enough galloping for one day. And back we swept across the crest of the Downs and I really was controlling him. His legs were moving under me as if in slow motion. I felt as if I were holding his power in a leash.

Which was how I got carried away. We finished the canter. We climbed the steep track down which we'd walked the horses on the outward route and started on the long, downward slope that led to the Forestry gate. Mio and I were in front, side by side with a girl on Iggy. We were talking and admiring the view when Iggy started to trot. Mio trotted too. No harm in that, I decided. Then Iggy started to canter. *Canter?* I thought. Going downhill? Well, his rider knew this stretch better than I did. No doubt it levelled out farther on.

So I let Mio canter too, confident that now I could control him. Only when Iggy's rider realised what he was doing she reined him and he stopped immediately —but when I tried to check Mio, he shook his head and went straight on.

Downhill . . . as straight as a skittle alley in reverse. He was gathering speed with every bound. I tried to turn him—he just raced on like a camel, his head pulled high and sideways against the reins. He couldn't see, and didn't care, where he was going. I had to let him loose or he'd have tripped himself up. I tried to turn him the other way, towards a patch of gorse and bracken. He didn't slacken speed. He'd have charged it, hidden holes and all. So I let him loose again and he raced exuberantly onwards, towards the Forestry gate at the bottom of the hill.

There, at last, I stopped him. I'd thought of turning him uphill just before the gate, where another track led up along the Forestry fence, but as I pulled on the left rein, so he gathered himself for the turn; obviously he wanted to go up there. Because it led to another stretch where he could gallop, I thought—so I ran him straight at the gate. He stopped a foot this side of it, as if on air-brakes, and began nonchalantly to crop the grass.

Gosh, he liked me riding him. Got on well together, didn't we? he snorted as the others appeared on the horizon.

Chapter Eight

Riding was becoming more popular. There was no doubt about that. The Hutchings had taken on additional horses to meet the demand and more and more local people were actually owning them. There were ponies in fields where there hadn't been any for years, hunters in long-disused stables, people in riding boots everywhere, hooves clip-clopping down the lane at every turn.

"Th'old Squire wouldn't half be pleased," said Father Adams, "to see all the hosses about again."

Th'old Squire, from what I'd heard of him, would more likely have had a fit. Fond of horses he might have been, but they were for the gentry, not for ordinary folk. The baker's daughter riding, and riding extremely well? "Gel," I can imagine him saying "ought to know her place."

The Squire was long before our time at the cottage, but he was still a legend in the village. How he'd pulled the cottagers' roofs off and used to have boxing matches with tramps, how he'd dam the stream to practise horse-jumping and to the devil with the labourers' wives' cooking. They used the water from the stream for household purposes in those days and it was highly inconvenient when he cut it off. "I suppose they were all right for cooking on Sundays, though," I said.

"The Squire'd have been in his pew in church then, not down the Valley jumping."

Father Adams, who'd been telling me all this, looked at me with scorn. "Th'old Squire go to church?" he said. "He always got drunk on Sunday mornings."

The Rector, it seemed, had remonstrated with him about the roofs and this was the Squire's reply. He got roaring drunk every Sunday morning thinking about the parson's impertinence and when the congregation arrived for morning service there he was, tweed-hatted, waving his stick, reeling about by the church porch ordering the villagers not to go in.

"Did they go in?" I asked. From what I'd heard the villagers of that generation had been pretty tough themselves. For a start no outsider could marry a girl from this village unless he could beat one of the natives in a kicking match. But it sounded as if it was asking for trouble to deliberately flout the Squire.

"Used to pretend to turn back and then go round the side and in through t'other door," said Father Adams. "What was more, th'old Squire knowed they done it. 'Twould have spoiled it for 'un if they hadn't, 'cause he used to wait there and swear at 'em again when they came out."

An odd mixture he'd been, by all accounts. This business of fighting with tramps, for instance . . . it seemed that the Squire, by temperament obviously a descendant of the Regency bucks, was proud of his prowess with his fists and liked to keep in practice. Having lost several good grooms because they got tired of being ordered to fight with him, while the villagers refused to a man . . . nobody lost their roof because they wouldn't fight, apparently, any more than they did for going to church ... he took to challenging any tramp who happened along to put the gloves on with him behind the stables. If the tramp beat the Squire he got a meal in the Moat House kitchen and a five pound-note for his pains. If the tramp lost, however—as some of them excusably thought they were meant to do—one of the grooms was called to boot him down the drive while the poor soul wondered where he'd gone wrong.

The story of the cottage roofs was a rum one, too. In the mid-1700s, it seemed, there'd been a tremendous demand for calamine, which was used, with copper, for the manufacture of brass. Our hills contained particularly good quality calamine and miners poured into the district from Wales, Cornwall, Yorkshire—hence the incorporation into local custom of the miners' traditional kicking matches.

Those who could, got homes in the main village. Those who couldn't, built their own. In the Valley mostly, where they raised a colony of stone cottages by the stream. On land belonging to the old Squire's great-grandfather, though they didn't worry about that. Neither did the Squire's great-grandfather, apparently. Probably he had an interest in the mining.

By the 1890s, however, when the Squire Father Adams remembered came into the inheritance, the calamine vein had long since run out and many of the miners had emigrated. Others had become farm labourers, still living in the cottages in the Valley, hiring themselves out for work on local farms and doing a considerable amount of poaching on the side. The Valley men, ex-miners and descendants of miners, prided themselves on their lawlessness.

Naturally it was the Squire's estate they poached on, living as they did on the edge of it. Fred Ferry's grandfather had been one of the gang and Fred often boasted about it. He told us once how they outwitted the gamekeeper when they took their haul to town.

Our cottage, it seemed, had been the collecting point. "Many a time," said Fred (he was in our sitting-room at the time; gazing with reverent awe at our ceiling) . . . "many a time, my granfer said, he'd seen thic beams hung solid with pheasants. Waiting for the night-time, when they'd take 'em off to Bristol."

Apparently the procedure was for the known poachers to congregate at the Rose and Crown. The gamekeeper, who lived in a cottage, now a ruin, in the Forest, used to call in for his nightly pint; one of the villagers used to press him to another; the gamekeeper, seeing all the suspects innocently playing dominoes or gossiping round the fire, thought it was safe and accepted . . . and another, and another, till he was pretty well squiffed while still, loyally remembering his duty, keeping a bleary eye on the poachers. Meanwhile the mile and a half of lane between us and the main road . . . up the hill, round the corner by the Rose and Crown, down past the church and the Moat House (no need to worry about the Squire; he could be depended on to be sozzled) was as alive with women and children carrying partridges or pheasants or rabbits as any smugglers' cliff path in Cornwall. Perhaps this was a Cornishman's idea. There were several Cornish miners in the Valley. And out on the road the carts were waiting with hooded lamps, to take the booty through the night to town, and when the gamekeeper, awash with cider, eventually rolled down the hill, our cottage

and the others merely showed innocently lamplit curtains.

Nobody was ever caught, presumably because of this double-take system where the game was trapped one night, kept through the day in our cottage and smuggled out while the poachers presented an en masse alibi, like a Pirates of Penzance chorus, up in the Rose and Crown. The goods were never discovered in our cottage because, as its occupant was neither a tenant nor an employee of the Squire, neither he nor his gamekeeper had any reason to call there—and probably wouldn't have dared to if they had. "Toughest of the lot he was, the bloke that lived in here," Fred Ferry informed us with satisfaction. "Granfer said he were built like an ox and always kept his kicking boots by his bed."

But the Squire obviously had his suspicions so he got together with his lawyer and they thought up a plan to take care of things. If anybody wonders why he didn't call the police, he probably did and the police refused to come. More than one constable, according to local history, got himself thrown down a calamine hole in the bad old days through arguing law with the miners.

So the cottagers were invited to a harvest home at which the lawyer explained the Squire's plans for their welfare. If they'd sign these papers, he told them, just to make everything legal, their cottages would be repaired by the estate and they needn't worry about the rent.

They'd never paid rent anyway but most of them signed, thinking they were on to a good thing, and the Squire duly kept his word, repairing windows, putting doors on privies, patching up ceilings when required ... until the occupant who'd signed the agreement died, when his heirs found the flaw in the deal. The occupancy didn't pass on to them. It terminated with the signatory's death. And then the bailiff turned them out and took the roof off.

It was one way of stopping the poaching and, as the Squire had no doubt planned, of ridding the Valley of its human population and letting it revert to shooting land. It was pretty successful, too. Only a handful of cottages—ours and Father Adams's among them—escaped the wholesale demolition. Our predecessor with the kicking boots had refused to sign the agreement and the others managed to outlive the Squire. His heir had been of a less ruthless disposition and allowed the survivors to remain. True to human nature it wasn't he who stood out in local memory, however, but the colourful, swashbuckling figure of the old Squire. Jumping his black mare over the stream, riding her to hounds, fighting with tramps behind the stables, careering round the lanes in his sledge. Even when they told the story of the cottage roofs they recounted it with proprietary pride. "He were a real old b." they'd say. "They don't make 'em like he nowadays."

Just as well, too, but the fact is that country people like having a squire around, if it's only to get revolutionary about, hold fêtes on his lawn, and be able to talk about him in the local and impress the Sunday-morning-pinters out from town. We didn't have one. The estate had long been sold. The Howells lived very quietly in the Moat House. "Tin't like the old days. Th'old Squire'd have made things hum," Fred Ferry and Father Adams were always saying.

Human—and particularly rural—nature being what it is, they were naturally the first to take exception when we did acquire a squire. A squiress, to be exact, and something of a proxy one. She didn't live in the local manor. She lived in the Tower House, well beyond the village, and took us under her copious wing from there.

We saw her first one afternoon when we'd had a lot of rain and the stream was running full spate. Father Adams was chatting with us at the cottage gate and Fred Ferry was grousing in the lane. The stream forms a ford across the lane beyond our wall and Fred had just jumped its swollen width and landed short. "Got me ruddy feet wet now," he said. "They ought to put pipes in here."

Over our dead bodies they would have. Badgers came to the ford to drink, and foxes, and all kinds of birds. Blackbirds, yellowhammers, long-tailed tits, wagtails . . . they all bathed there and dried off in the lilac tree by the coalhouse. With two Siamese cats yattering at them through the window, of course, but the birds knew when they were safe. A blue or seal-point nose had only to appear round the door and the birds were over in the big nut-tree in our woods like a flash. Flipping their tails in derision at the cats and busily preening their feathers.

The ford has history to it, too. The Romans and Danes had ridden through it—one of the tracks to the camp led up from there. Fred Ferry had fallen in it countless times as a boy—he was always telling us about that. Over his dead body, also, would anybody have altered it, but it was second nature to him to grumble. Which he was doing in full measure when the woman from the Tower House came round the corner.

She was accompanied by two small boys and a couple of labrador dogs. The dogs took off like greyhounds after a wood pigeon which was picking up grit in the lane, the boys made for the ford like elephants stampeding a water-hole, and the woman from the Tower House stood there and shouted at the lot of them.

"Beuteh! Blaze!" she yelled refinedly after the dogs. "Jeremeh . . . James . . . Come out of there at once!" she ordered. Nobody obeyed her, the bedlam continued and Fred Ferry said once more that this lot ought to be piped.

"Oh we *live* heah . . . over at the Towah House . . . we're *used* to it," trilled the woman. Not having the least idea who Fred was but obviously determined to sustain a picture of carefree country living.

"I bain't then," said Fred. "Me feet be wet."

"Oh rahlly . . . how dreadful . . . BEUTEH!" bawled the woman. "I'll mention it to my husband. He may be able to do something about it," she said in an authoritative voice to Fred.

He didn't, of course. Even before she'd got her charges

under control, Fred, his ears geranium with excitement, was on his way up the hill like a homing cart-horse. Stolid, seemingly unhurried—and hardly able to wait, if we knew anything about him, to get the news to the Rose and Crown . . . that She from th' Tower House was poking her nose in, wanting to put the stream under the road. When her husband enquired in due course whether there was anything he could do to help there were plenty of people to tell him nay. By that time the ford had become as precious as the Koh-i-noor and the district would have defended it with its life.

She from th' Tower House, as she was thereafter known to us all, certainly did her best. She tried to get in with the right people—making discreet enquiries, which went round the village as if by tom-tom, as to who the right people were. That we weren't among them was made very clear to me one day. "I heah you keep cats," she bellowed at me over the wall. "Can never understand what people see in them myself—but of course *I* was brought up with dogs and horses."

"Don't need a telescope to see that," muttered Father Adams who was helping me weed the garden.

"What did he say?" demanded the lady in the lane.

"Er . . . nothing. Nice weather, isn't it?" I said.

She'd already managed to upset Father Adams. He'd been sawing up logs in his garden one morning when she happened along, dogs, children and all as usual, and offered him an old apple tree they'd cut down at the Tower House. Father Adams had accepted. He—and we—like log fires in winter and apple wood makes particularly fragrant burning.

"Come over and speak to the gardenah about it," she continued. "He'll arrange when you can have it.

We were going to use it for the bonfah on Guy Fawkes night but it seems a shame if someone could do with it."

It was bad enough to suggest that Father Adams burned wood because he was needy. To tell him to apply to the gardener, however—who happened to be Ern Biggs from the next village and Father Adams's particular bête noir on account of Father Adams did odd-job gardening himself and considered Ern to be an interloper—added such insult to injury that the old boy turned his back on her, didn't collect the apple tree, and when in due course, as was no doubt inevitable, she too appeared on a horse, took every opportunity of disconcerting her.

She did rather ask for it. Instead of contenting herself with one horse she appeared in splendour with two. Riding one, leading the other, her dogs trespassing in everybody's gardens. Her husband didn't ride, her children were too small—nobody could understand why she had two of them. Unless she thought it looked more impressive and what a squire's wife would do.

It was impressive all right. You could hear the procession coming as far away as the Rose and Crown. The clattering hooves, the shouted greetings to people, the bellowing for the dogs to come to heel. "Sounds," Father Adams would comment witheringly, "like a whole ruddy hunt by herself. It's a wonder to I she don't get herself a horn."

When she eventually appeared in the Valley Father Adams was usually in position by our gate. She might not be going down by his cottage but he could be sure of her having to come past ours. And there, while I mentally wilted, he passed comment to the world at large.

"In my time," he observed loudly on one occasion (I was on my hands and knees behind the wall; invisibly, I hoped, weeding the path) " 'twas only grooms that took spare hosses out for exercise, but I 'spose they can't afford 'em nowadays."

"Whass reckon she wants two on 'em for?" he enquired another time when she'd just gone by. "Think she be practising for a circus—goin' to ride 'em one foot on each when she gets down in the Valley?"

It was Fred Ferry who aided him in his greatest coup, however. This time they were both at our gate when she went past . . . turning to stare at her under their hat brims which was pretty disconcerting for a start.

"Whass reckon she wants two for, Fred?" demanded Father Adams in a voice that could be heard at the top of the Valley.

"Thass a spare for when she gets the one she's ridin' wore out," said Fred Ferry equally loudly.

"Wore out?" asked Father Adams. "Do she ride 'em as hard as that then?"

"Ah," said Fred stentorially. "Thee'st should see her up on the Downs."

Up on the Downs—as Fred well knew, having seen her, and as she knew Fred knew because she couldn't possibly have missed seeing him—she did what she always did. Rode at a walk.

The idea of her needing a relief horse had me nearly in stitches but those two stood there as solemn as owls.

"Takes some ridin' to do that, Fred," Father Adams broadcast in the direction of her departing back.

"Ah," said Fred. "But thee hassn't seen her like I have. 'Tis a wonder to I she don't have three."

Chapter Nine

We didn't see her in the Valley for quite a while after that, though stories of the new regime at the Tower House continued to filter down to us. Ern Biggs related one of them at the Rose and Crown, as a result of which Father Adams actually bought him a pint.

Apparently a lot of alterations had been done to the place—central heating put in, parquet floors in place of flagstones, a tarmac drive instead of the mellow old yellow-mossed gravel. And when it was all done, except for a final small stretch of the tarmac, various friends were invited for a viewing. They arrived en bloc one Saturday morning for lunch, while Ern was still digging one of the flower beds, and they got out of their cars and gushed around, commenting on what had been done.

"Oh look! They've got a gardener!" squealed one. "Double glazing!" screeched another. "That must be Bertie's new grass cutter," said a third, pointing farther up the drive towards the lawn. At the end of which, awaiting the return of the tarmac men on Monday, was a large, brass-plated steam-roller . . . and while by this time we were all very well aware that Bertie and his wife always had the biggest, best and most expensive of everything, the idea of Bertie trundling round the Tower House lawns with a mower the size of a steam-roller was the joke of the village for weeks.

What intrigued us, however, watching the world go past our garden gate, was how this business of one rider with two horses seemed to be catching on. We'd been amused by it at first, looking on it as ridiculous affectation. But the number of riders who now began to appear in the Valley leading a second horse—really it was quite incredible. Whether it was a new kind of status symbol... two horses being even better than two cars... whether it suddenly struck people who did have two that this was a time-saving way of exercising them... coupled, no doubt, with the sort of copying craze of children wanting roller skates or pink hair-ribbon... the fact remained that while the instigator herself remained absent from the Valley for quite a while, two horses at a time were definitely now "in".

Mums with children away at school rode one pony and led the other. Somebody with a couple of hunters came clattering down the hill with those. Even Mrs. Howell once (but only once) appeared riding her grey mare, Molly, and resolutely leading Troika. The position changed dramatically once they were through the Forestry gate. Troika went up the track like a kite with a tail, towing Molly and Mrs. Howell behind him.

Eventually the craze died down a bit. Not before we'd fielded quite a few loose-running horses in the lane, however, lead-ropes dangling and their embarrassed erstwhile handlers frantically in pursuit. And not before one enterprising child had the idea of trying it out with Annabel.

It so happened that there was, in a village some four miles away, a donkey called Charlie. Annabel had met him once before—when, in the summer holidays, a crowd of children had escorted him over to see her. It was one of the scenes of which, for us, country life consists. Annabel, posed on the hillock in her paddock from which she watches everything, surveying their approach with the dignity of a small but superior queen. Charlie, unable to believe his eyes when he saw her, braying hopefully at her through the gate. Annabel, still as a statue on her hillock, regarding him silently from under her fringe.

When she wouldn't come down to meet him the children led Charlie off down the lane again. Four times, struck by a thought which stopped him dead in his tracks, he turned round and came back for another look. Each time his pigtailed rider, aided by the other children pushing, got him headed for home again, while our temptress stood complacently on her hillock like Helen watching Paris set sail from Troy.

Only when it was obvious that the procession was finally under way—was in fact just about to vanish round the curve by Father Adams's cottage—did Annabel at last unbend. "Woo-hoo-hoo-hoo" she bawled, raising her head like a trumpet. And Charlie came back again.

I was struck by the patience and tenacity of Charlie's rider. I couldn't have done that with Mio. The way she reined him, turned him, put her heels to him and Charlie, albeit under protest, obeyed and went the other way. I also knew Annabel, however, and when, while this fashion for leading horses was still with us, the entourage turned up again, asking this time if they could take Annabel with them because Hazel wanted to lead her with Charlie . . . regretfully I had to say no. Annabel caused enough trouble when we took her out on her own. She and Charlie in tandem would have cleared the Forest tracks like a fire-engine. Besides, I said to Charles, people might think we were doing it deliberately. Making fun of all the riders trotting importantly round with two horses.

We did, of course, take Solomon and Sheba out together. We'd been doing it since they were kittens. They, when we looked back on it, had been enough of a dual handful. Vanishing into cornfields, going up trees . . . the times we'd had to come back for a ladder. Now though, even as we watched them meandering up the lane and remarked how sprightly they looked, we wondered in our heart of hearts how long the pattern would continue. They were growing old. Sheba, we knew, had kidney trouble. Yet it was impossible to imagine the cottage without them.

As impossible as it was to imagine a time when Iggy and Mio would no longer race each other along the Forest tracks, manes flying, necks outstretched in eagerness, slim legs drumming an urgent tattoo that lifted one's heart just to hear it.

And yet, all too soon, it came. I couldn't believe it when I went up to the stables one morning and Mrs. Hutchings told me that Iggy was dead. "Iggy?" I said. "But he's only young . . . Iggy can't be dead."

He was. He was lying in his stable, his long chestnut legs outstretched. With him, crying unashamedly, was the man who would have ridden him that morning.

The futility of it hits me even now. Iggy was seven—young for a horse—and there hadn't been a thing wrong with him. He'd been out the previous day as usual. Mrs. Hutchings had ridden him on his last ride. He'd gone, he and Mio, like the wind, she said. She'd taken them out across the Downs. She was glad of that. He'd always liked it up there.

And he'd come back, been put into his loose box, unsaddled and fed. And there'd been something sharp in his food that had penetrated his stomach wall and killed him. A chance in a million, the Vet said after the post mortem. It could have been as little as a splinter of wood in his hay—they never knew exactly what it was. It if had gone through lengthways it wouldn't have done any harm, but it had turned sideways and punctured the stomach lining. There must have been a brief moment of pain and then he'd dropped like a stone . . . so quickly that the rug he wore at night hadn't even been disturbed.

So, so senselessly, passed Iggy. The great-hearted, beautiful Prince Igor. Friend of my friend Mio, who was now given Iggy's stable.

Only temporarily, said Lynn. Until they could get a replacement for Iggy. But she couldn't bear to see the blank half-door at which Iggy had stood for so long, his inquisitive golden head watching all that went on in the yard. Turning every now and then to check that Mio's head was out of the next one and that old dun-ears hadn't stolen a march on him and got taken out on his own.

So for a while Mio looked out over Iggy's door and though he obviously missed Iggy on the ride . . . looking round for him when we stopped, gazing expectantly back along the track, his ears pricked, when we cantered, for the hoofbeats that should have been there alongside him . . . one thing Mio did appreciate was having Iggy's stable.

It was bigger than his. All the loose boxes were roomy but there were two that were particularly large. Built for the two tall thoroughbreds, Iggy and Jasper, who were kept in all the winter except when they were working, as opposed to the ponies who, if the weather wasn't too bad, preferred to be out on the hill.

Mio stayed in all the winter too, but, being smaller than they were on account of so much Arab in him, he had a slightly smaller loose box—No. 2 in the top horses' block on the left-hand side of the yard. Iggy had been No. 1. Jasper was No. 3. To be moved up into the top place—gosh, it made Mio feel important. He emerged, when he was led out for a ride, as if he were the stable king. Until Zaboine arrived as replacement for Iggy and Mio went back to being No. 2.

If ever a horse sulked, Mio did. Obviously Zaboine needed the bigger stable. He was a 16-hand Russian, practically identical with Iggy. That was why Lynn had bought him, apart from his being good. She said it was like having Iggy back again.

Not to Mio it wasn't. He went at the newcomer with his ears back and his teeth bared if they were in the yard together. Pretending to be Ig, he said... *He* knew, if the others didn't. Why didn't he go Home? We didn't want strangers round here... taking Other People's stables, he said, lunging at him again.

I had made a fuss of Mio from the moment I first rode him, talking to him, asking how he was, rubbing his nearside foreleg. Not that there was anything wrong with it. Just that Mio liked to have it rubbed and held it up as soon as he saw me.

It was a habit that had been started by Lynn. Mio, she said, was a great baby. He fussed if his back was cold when his saddle was put on. (He did indeed; he used to go round the stable yard, when I got on him on cold mornings, sinking spectacularly in the middle.) He fussed even more when he'd been clipped, which is done, in winter, to working horses so that if they sweat after a gallop they don't have wet, hairy coats on them to give them chills when they cool down again. I wondered what was wrong when, coming down the drive one morning, Mio started to squeal and fidget his bottom. It felt as if he was bucking. This, I thought, I couldn't risk. If Mio went bucking through the village, I bet I'd come off in the pond.

I mentioned it to Lynn. It was all right, she assured me. He'd forget about it in a minute. It was just that he'd been clipped. Putting his saddle on made his back tickle and, being Mio, he made a fuss about it. He said he had a Sensitive Skin.

So sensitive that Lynn always stretched his forelegs after his girth-strap was fastened, to make sure his stomach hadn't got pinched in the webbing. The others,

she said, would have taken it in their stride. Mio would have hit the heavens.

Thus evolved the ceremony of Mio standing in the yard after he'd been saddled while Lynn stretched each of his forelegs in turn. Solicitously, obviously very much concerned about himself, he held each hoof up for her to do it. And as I had no more sense than to stroke the uplifted leg on my side and ask if that was where it hurt . . . after that, every time he saw me, up came the leg for my inspection as well.

In the yard originally. But after Zaboine came and Mio went back to No. 2, whenever I went to get him out, up would go his foreleg in his loose box. Got Cramp in it, he said. Couldn't move a Step till I'd rubbed it. This stable wasn't big enough to swing a Mouse in. After which, regardless of the fact that there was at least a couple of yards clear behind him, he'd turn to stand with his face close against the side wall and sway his head from side to side. See that? he demanded. Wasn't even room for his Nose. Couldn't I Complain and get him back in No. 1?

He had bags of room. What was more, once he was out in the yard his troubles vanished like chaff before the wind. It was me going to ride him? We'd show that new horse This Time, said the sway of his hindquarters as we went down the drive.

We did too. Never have I been carted so consistently as in those weeks when they first had Zab. Up hill, down dale, round corners. . . . One corner I remember particularly. Lynn, in those early days, was trying Zaboine out; making sure he was safe for less accomplished riders; holding him back to see if he'd try to fight her control. "You can go on if you like," she said on this occasion. "But slow down when you get to the corner and wait for the rest of us there."

We went. Off up through the glade, leaving the others behind us, savouring the special magic of a summer morning in the quiet places of the hills. A fox ran across the track ahead of us—probably it had been basking in the sun at the wood-edge; there was one which did that sometimes on the hillside behind the cottage. A couple of partridge whirred out of the bracken and flew clumsily low into the woods. A pheasant shrilled inside the wood, raucous as a peacock. Yellow butterflies played lazily in warm hollows formed by the brambles. Mio sped through it like Pegasus, loving every moment of it. Out in front, weren't we? said the eager tilt of his ears. Could I feel how powerful his legs were, going on this springy turf?

I could indeed. And for the moment I, too, was enjoying it. I had the balance of Mio now. I had no fear of his speed. I always wondered whether I'd stop him, mind you, but right now we were going uphill. . . .

At that moment we reached the top of the glade and came out on the level. We could go Faster on this lot, said Mio, suiting his action to his words. I remembered the adjunct about sitting down, however, and giving and taking with the reins. . . .

It worked. I managed to slow him. To a fast trot, not a walk, but it worked. I relaxed a little. He was slowing to a stop, I thought. He knew we had to wait at the corner.

Like heck he did. We were going downhill once more—always my bugbear with Mio. As if he couldn't help it he began to increase his speed. Whoops . . . it was this incline . . . making him Run, he said. Before I could do anything about it we were going like mad again. Stop at the corner? We went round it like a catherine wheel. We were showing that Zaboine, weren't we? he said. He knew I could stay on him if I Wanted to, even if it *was* an abrupt right turn.

Fortunately it was also uphill again and this time, near the top, I stopped him. Even he had had enough by now. This bit was as steep as a mountain.

Where one goes up one has to come down again, however, and in no time he'd recovered his wind. And, of course, he was all keyed up, after the exhilarating gallop we'd had. So, on the next downhill slope, he started off again, this time accompanied by Snowball who for once, though it was a weekday, had a rider. A small, somewhat nervous woman who was just the right weight for him.

She was small but she couldn't half scream. This time I was determined to stop Mio and I did, turning him sideways, his forelegs rearing up in protest, against a high bank of bilberries. But Mrs. Dickson shot on downhill on Snowball, shrieking "Help" and clinging to his neck. He was going like a little grey train, his small legs working like pistons. Down and round the slopes of the switchback-like track that wound steeply down to the Valley.

We watched helplessly from the top. It was no use anyone chasing after her. Another horse racing from behind would have only made Snowball go the faster. Then two other horses appeared beyond her, coming in the opposite direction. We held our breath. Would they crash? What would happen? "Help! Help!" shrieked Mrs. Dickson.

It was all right. It was the woman from the Tower

House. Walking her horses at a snail's pace as usual, so there wasn't any bother about stopping them. Snowball slid to a halt when he saw that his way was blocked. Mrs. Dickson fell off with relief. The woman from the Tower House had a fine old time telling her how she'd saved her. "Good job I was able to stop my two," she bawled. "They've both got mouths of iron."

Mio, who'd been the cause of it all, looked down at them with perked ears and snorted. Must have been that Zab frightened Snowball, he said. He wondered why we didn't send him back. Fancy old Snowball getting out of control, too. Good thing *he* wasn't like that.

Chapter Ten

That was the autumn that Solomon died. Sheba, we knew, had had kidney trouble for years, but Solomon had always seemed so fit and bounding. Only a few weeks previously he had chased another cat up the hill as if he were a little Camargue bull himself, whip-tail flying, his long black legs kicking exuberantly out behind him. Afraid of cars, I had run after him and

brought him back down to the cottage balanced, as he loved to be, on my shoulder. If I hadn't Stopped him ... if I wasn't holding him by his Tail ... he'd have chased that other cat right out of the village, he assured me. Fourteen and a half and he acted as if he were four. There were years and years yet, I told myself.

And now he was gone. It seemed that he'd had kidney trouble too, but his system had compensated for it and we hadn't known it. He'd been ill for only a week. We were thankful for that. But now, when I rode past the spot out across the hills where once I'd got off and carried him home, there were three shadows to travel with me ... his, Rory's and Iggy's. I stroked Mio's neck. "Years yet for you," I whispered. But always, always, time was passing.

Always there is heartache when we let animals into our lives, because we love them and they die, leaving us to mourn them. Sometimes there is sadness even worse than that. At least when they die we know their ending.

The other kind of heartache I witnessed one evening the following May. It was the Monday of the Spring Bank Holiday. It had been a beautiful day, with a heat haze over the hills and a cuckoo calling persistently down the Valley. There'd been lots of walkers about, admiring the apple blossom in the orchard and the stream bank yellow with celandines and the bluebells in the woods opposite the cottage. Now they had gone, their holiday over, and though we'd been glad to share the Valley with them it was nice to have it to ourselves again.

Nice, too, to think of the happy day they'd had... the people who'd picnicked on the hillside, the children who'd cuddled Annabel, the ones who'd paddled and played in the ford. Charles, keeping an eye on their dam-building activities (otherwise we were likely to wake up next morning and find we had a lake instead of a lawn), had shown them the bees collecting water from the stream... flying down from the hive in the orchard, queuing patiently on the stone they used as a jetty, flying back up—heavy now with the weight of the water which they used, mixed with pollen, to build the brood cells. "Why don't they use little buckets?" one small girl enquired. "And pull them up on a pulley," suggested her engineering-minded brother. We'd spent quite a while enlarging on that idea... one bee busily turning a windlass and buckets the size of thimbles going up by bee ski-lift to the hive. . . .

And now Charles was closing up the greenhouse and I was watering the paeonies, watched through the cottage window by an indignant Siamese kitten. Seeley, successor to Solomon, who'd brought happiness back to us, too, and comfort to our dear old Sheba, though you wouldn't have thought it from the way he was bawling now about we were Horrid to him and he Didn't Like Us and why wouldn't we let him Come Out?

On account of it was getting near dusk and there could be foxes about, as a matter of fact. There was the dog-fox, lighter than usual, the colour of winter bracken, who sunned himself sometimes up on the wood-edge. He knew us and we knew him, but we didn't know how he felt about little cats. There was the one, too, we'd seen sitting in the Forestry lane one night. About a hundred yards up, looking interestedly down at the cottage. The same one, Charles thought, that he'd seen trotting past our gate in full light one evening—he still hadn't got over that. He was looking at the fish-pool and he'd happened to glance through the gate and there, coming round the corner, was a fox. He'd have thought it was a dog, he said, if it hadn't been for its colour, trotting openly down the road and then across the ford and past our gate. It glanced in at Charles as it passed and pattered unhurriedly onwards . . . a young one, a magnificent russet, its great brush feathering the dust. Had the light-coloured one—his father, maybe—told him he needn't worry about us? That we considered it was his Valley as well as ours and delighted to see him passing through it?

Seeley wouldn't have considered it the fox's valley, however. He'd already got himself bitten by an adder, trying to clear the place of those, and we'd rushed him, screaming in agony, to the Vet. Fortunately the adder had struck him in his paw—Seeley always experimentally poked everything—and the venom had entered at the furthest point from his heart. He'd got over that—but a fox, as I was always lecturing him, would be a different kettle of fish to poke. He had to stay *in*, I told him now. It was the foxes' time to be about. But I'd be in in a moment and we'd play with his ball with a bell on.... It wasn't Fair... I didn't Love him, Seeley bawled tearfully through the window.

I did. To me he was Solomon all over again and when at that moment a girl went past on a pony... stroking its neck, leaning forward to whisper to it, ambling slowly up the hill in the dusk... what a wonderful world it was, I thought. The Valley, the Spring, a Siamese kitten—that girl with her pony, ambling homewards. What a day to remember *she'd* probably had, the two of them out across the hills.

A day to remember indeed, but not in the way I imagined. A few minutes later the girl rode back again—a little forlorn-looking, it struck me. Could I tell her the time? she asked. Nine o'clock, I said. She rode slowly on up towards the Hazells. She drifted back a second time and asked if she could use our phone. She'd arranged to meet a friend here, she told me. But the friend hadn't turned up. She was supposed to be bringing a picnic. At this time of night? my mental alarm bell registered.

She was, I guessed, about fifteen years old. She looped her pony's reins over the gatepost and came in and dialled a number in a village some miles away. When she asked for Betty and—obviously being asked who was calling—hesitantly replied "Miss Smith," I was even more certain there was something wrong. Fifteen year olds don't call themselves "Miss" when phoning their friends' homes—and apparently Betty wasn't there anyway. "It doesn't matter," said the girl, slowly putting down the receiver. She seemed to be on the verge of tears.

"What will you do now?" I asked. "It's getting too dark to take a pony on the roads in safety."

"Somebody's coming over with a horsebox," she said. "I'll ride up and wait at the end of the lane."

I didn't like it at all. There hadn't been any mention of a horsebox on the phone. But I couldn't very well prevent her from going. She got on her pony and rode off up the lane while I went to tell the story to Charles. Ten minutes later we walked to the end of the lane to check. There was no sign of the girl or the pony. Maybe she'd been right about the horsebox, said Charles. Perhaps it had been fixed beforehand....

I still had a feeling of uneasiness however and when, around one o'clock next morning, I woke to bright moonlight and the sound, which had penetrated my sleep, of a horse's shoes clattering on stones, I had no doubt as to who it was. I woke Charles. "It's that girl," I whispered urgently. "She's out in the lane right now."

We threw on some clothes and shot down and out into the lane. There was a riderless pony outside Annabel's stable. With a huddled heap on the verge at the pony's feet... I don't think we've ever run faster.

It was the girl all right. Not injured, as we'd feared. Just crouched there in an abandonment of despair.

We brought her indoors, put the pony on the lawn, turned the porch-light on so that anyone looking for him and his rider would see him. Then, plying the girl with tea and sandwiches, we got to the bottom of the mystery.

Her name was Angela and she'd run away from home because her parents were going to sell her pony. "They said he cost a lot and I wasn't looking after him properly," she said, the tears dropping on to her sandwiches. "I hadn't cleaned out his stable. I meant to, only there was my homework and everything.... But I just couldn't live without Jinty."

I didn't suppose they'd meant it, I said encouragingly. Parents did say things like that when they were cross.

"Oh no." She shook her head. "A dealer was coming for him this morning. He came and looked at him yesterday. I couldn't let Jinty go and never know where he was. So I got up at five and brought him away."

She'd had the idea of hiding with him out in our hills. Her friend Betty had promised to bring her food. She'd thought she might get a job on a farm—somewhere where they'd let her keep Jinty. Only plans that seem so simple when one first thinks them out tend to crumble when put to the test. Especially when one is a child, and despairing and cold, and one hasn't eaten all day.

She'd tried to sleep under the pine trees farther up the Valley, but she'd had to stay awake holding Jinty's reins. She'd forgotten to bring a tether rope and she was afraid he'd wander away. So she'd come back to our shed. She'd noticed it the previous evening. It had a door on it and she'd thought she could shut Jinty in. Then she'd found there was a donkey in it and she'd just lain down and cried. She supposed we were very cross with her, she said.

Cross with her indeed. "I'd have done the same myself,' I told her and she looked at me in amazement. "If anybody was going to take away *my* animals," I said. "So would I," Charles firmly assured her.

That was what I told her mother when I rang to say she was safe and would they like to come over and fetch her. The mother, once she'd gasped with relief and said that her husband was still out looking for her, was very concerned about my opinion. "It isn't like Angela at all," she said. "Not to worry us like this. She's always been so sensible—such a good girl. And I'm sure we've given her everything."

Everything except the security of knowing that the pony she loved was hers for always—though to be fair I could also see the parents' side of the picture. An animal is a living thing. It has to be looked after. It can't be left till tomorrow, like cleaning a pair of shoes.

"She'll look after him," I said. "That pony is her world. I promised her I'd ask you to let her keep him."

"We didn't realise he meant so much to her," she said. "I'll talk it over with her father."

She didn't have to. I'd just put down the phone when a car came down the hill and stopped. There was a horse-box behind it and a man and a girl in jodhpurs got out. They'd spotted the pony on the lawn under the porch-light. Obviously this was the search party.

"Is she all right?" her father called as I opened the door. "We've been searching for her all day. This was the only place left to look. . . ."

"She's fine except that she's very tired. Don't be cross with her," I said.

He tried to be. "A fine chase *you've* given us, my girl," he said as he came into the sitting-room. And then she was in his arms, and he was ruffling her hair, and now we had two of them crying.

I made some more tea. It was two in the morning by this time. And then we loaded Jinty into the horse-box. It belonged to the other girl, Jean, who'd apparently taught Angela to ride, and had volunteered to help look for the runaways. "I've got to be up at six," she told me as she fastened the bolts on the tail-board. "I'm taking an all-day trekking party out. Why on earth I went in for horses...."

Angela's father thanked us again. He asked if there was anything he could do to repay us. "Let her keep Jinty," we said.

He did. We've seen her many times since then, riding in convoy through the Valley. She comes with Jean and her riding club. She handles Jinty very well. They always stop for a chat at the gate and Annabel woo-hoo-hoo's from the hillside ... Annabel's way of greeting people she remembers. We never refer to the night she ran away but Annabel obviously always reminds Jinty. Remember that night he woke us up? she bawls. And we gave him some of her Hay?

That story had a happy ending, but there are so many that don't. Sometimes it is the horse that suffers, because its owner does get tired of it. One sees them standing in fields, lonely, unvisited ... until one day the dealer's van arrives, or maybe the knackers. That is why, I always say, I wouldn't have a horse myself. I could never bear to part with it and risk it ending like that. I would have to keep it for ever.

"What about Mio?" Charles enquired. "You think

as much of him as if he were your own."

I do, but he is as safe with the Hutchings as if he were mine. And he has, I hope, years and years yet.

Chapter Eleven

It was thanks to Mio and Annabel that we were eventually so successful with badger-watching. Not, I regret to say, as the result of combined effort on their parts. Nothing would have been more wonderful than to have ridden out over the hills on Mio with Annabel trotting jauntily at my side and, if it had been possible, Seeley perched in front of me on the saddle.

Alas for that little daydream. . . . Horses on the whole love donkeys. They seem to regard them as some sort of equine infant. The ones that like Annabel drool

over her like besotted aunts and refuse to go by until they've nudged noses, while Annabel stands there, eyes modestly lowered, her bottom lip pouting demurely. There is no happy medium, however. Horses either love donkeys or they practically climb trees when they see them. Of the Hutchings' fourteen there were two that were dead scared of Annabel and one— you could have bet on it—was Mio. The other was Halberdier, who was also scared of mice; he used to whinny and pick his feet up if he saw one. Maybe he thought Annabel was some sort of mouse too—he was so huge, it was like Gulliver with a Lilliputian.

Mio, however—goodness knew why he disliked donkeys, but he used to snort and walk sideways when he saw her. Not just with me on him. He'd always done it. He acted as though she was going to attack him.

He was scared enough before I rode him—when all she did was raise her head from grazing as he passed and regard him with a contemplative, cud-chewing stare. When I started riding him, however, and the view she presented was of an intimidatingly hostile rear, I could understand his apprehension. It intimidated me too. She Knew I was on him, was the message. She wasn't Speaking to me. And if we came any nearer she'd Kick him.

This happened when she was in her field (in which case she stood with her back ostentatiously turned as we went past); when she was on her tether rope in the Forest (in which event she got as near to the track as her rope would allow and stood with her bottom to us from there); even when she was grazing way up the hillside under the wood-edge, where we had to peer upwards to see her but, to register her disapproval, she turned her back as we passed just the same.

In the circumstances there wasn't much likelihood of Mio ever nuzzling noses with her and his contribution to our badger-watching activities was that it was on him, riding through a distant part of the Forest, I noticed one day that an old sett was in use again.

We hadn't been up there for ages. We'd thought the sett was deserted and it was a long way to walk to look at empty holes. Now, from Mio's back, I had a commanding view into the wood and it looked as if a badger estate builder had moved in. Heaps of discarded bedding material, fresh earth turned out of several of the holes... many more holes than I'd ever seen before. Somebody'd apparently gone berserk and tunnelled exuberantly out under the roadway; there were even a couple of holes coming up in that. Each of them had a sawn-off section of tree-trunk stuffed down it, no doubt at the behest of an equally berserk Forestry Commission manager. This was a track built specially for the use of fire engines in an emergency and it wasn't exactly helpful to have badger holes in it.

Normally, of course, the Forestry Commission has no objection to badgers—even to the extent of putting special gates like cat-doors in the Forestry fences, so that the animals can use their ancient tracks undisturbed. Here, the thwarted tunneller had re-directed his energies to positively peppering the verge at the side of the road with holes. The purpose of this Charles and I were to see for ourselves one summer's evening. That morning, on Mio, the scene had the appearance of an empty stage.

A stage waiting, nevertheless, for its actors to appear. One was conscious of a definite presence, even if the striped-faced performers were at that moment snoring underground, with one of them dreaming of digging holes as big as bomb-craters and fire-engines falling into them by the dozen.

It was a fascinating place. Often in the following weeks I rode through there with Mrs. Hutchings and noted the progress of the digging. One night Charles and I walked up with a couple of friends, getting there just before dusk and waiting at the edge of the wood in the hope of seeing the badgers come out. After a while a white-striped head appeared briefly in one of the roadside holes, sniffed the air thoughtfully, like a

tea-taster, then disappeared again. It hadn't seemed alarmed so we waited patiently on, hoping for it to reappear. Only a good hour later did someone think of looking into the depths of the wood with binoculars —to see, silhouetted at the far end of the aisles of trees, where it was lighter, a positive procession of badgers going on. Low-slung, trundling black outlines disappearing over the horizon. No doubt laughing their heads off at us, waiting to see them come out by their front doors, while they, nipping under the forest floor via their underground passages, were quietly slipping out by the back.

We went up several times that summer. Never did we catch more than a passing glimpse of a badger. A flash of white in an entrance hole; a big one, with a smaller one behind it, crossing far ahead of us on the track; the sound—frustrating, because we realised how near we'd been to seeing it—of a badger, disturbed while drinking at the stream beyond the sett, crashing away into the undergrowth.

This was the way we'd read it was, of course. One has to have patience with badgers. Be prepared to stay out all night to see them . . . only somehow we didn't fancy that.

And so it was that one evening the following Spring, resigned to the fact that we'd never be proper badger-watchers but fascinated by them just the same, we took Annabel up there for a walk to see how the sett was getting on. If we'd been proper badger-watchers, of course, we'd never have dreamed of taking her. For that pursuit one wants silence, not a donkey making as much noise as she can. Galloping the Forest paths like a Derby runner, stopping to tear at clumps of grass with the sound of rending calico, snorting at frequent intervals so that we won't forget she's there.

"We won't see anything with her along," I said as we rounded the corner above the sett. "But at least we can tell if they've been active. I'll just tie her up down the side lane to graze so we can go in and look at the holes."

With which I took her down the grassy sunken side-lane which ran between the sett and a patch of undergrowth on the left and even as I plodded downwards, my gumboots swishing heavily through the grass, there was a flurry among the pine trees in the sett itself and a badger dived down one of the holes.

We could hardly believe it. As early as this in the evening—it was quite a while yet till dusk. The noise we'd been making talking, and Annabel thumping along like an elephant with clogs on. . . . Just our luck, we said. If we hadn't brought her this might have been a very good night for viewing. Oh well, we might as well stand there for a while and let her have a feed. We could just be lucky and see a badger look out.

So we mounted the bank into the pine wood and I got behind a tree. Charles stood out in an open patch, not even bothering to take cover. No point, he said, after all the noise we'd made talking. And there was Annabel tearing at the grass as if she was starving and looking interestedly about her as she chewed, her ears whipping about in semaphore signals that even the shortest-sighted badger could hardly miss. . . . Her big white nose, too, standing out like a door-knocker and every now and then that derisive snort.

Whether the badgers thought she was a deer feeding, however—there were one or two, we knew, in the Forest. Whether they recognised her scent as that of an animal—not to be feared and of course it would cover ours. Whether donkeys have a tranquillising effect on all creatures—they use them, after all, to calm nervous racehorses. . . . All I know is that within minutes of taking up position in that wood, Charles and I within feet of each other, Annabel a few yards away at the edge of the lane, an adult badger and three cubs emerged from a hole just ahead of us and the cubs began to disport themselves among the trees.

Disport is the only word. It was like the Enchanted Wood scene in a pantomime—when, before the humans appear, sprites flit soft-footed on to the dim-lit stage and dance in magical silence. The cubs chased each other, jumped each other, rolled in combat like puppies ... the adult, obviously the mother, keeping guard. Everything was as hushed as if it were in a dream. One move and the stage would be empty again.

One move on our part, that is. The other badgers didn't even bother to look when, following considerable rustling in the undergrowth on the other side of the sunken lane, a big boar badger emerged. He glided close to the ground, silently now and smoothly, as if he ran by clockwork. It was the nearest I had ever been to a badger. He crossed the lane, glancing interestedly at Annabel and came up into the wood, approaching us along a narrow, well-trodden path—on which, I suddenly realised, Charles was standing!

The badger was still looking sideways at Annabel. Any moment I expected to see him collide with Charles. Charles said afterwards, having read that badgers have jaws like spring-traps, he was just wondering whether he ought to withdraw his toes from the line of fire ... when the badger reverted his gaze to the front, saw a pair of legs bang in front of him, jumped like a startled rabbit and was past Charles and down a hole in a flash.

The others disappeared simultaneously. The enchanted wood was deserted. Just for a second—and then, quite incredibly, a badger came out of another hole. Even nearer to me this time. I could practically have touched him. But he wasn't in the least concerned with me. Rearing on his hind legs, obviously consumed with curiosity, he was craning, like a spectator at a football match with somebody tall in front of him, through the trees in the direction of Annabel.

It was, I was sure of it, the one which had nearly fallen over Charles. There was something about him one could recognise. An intrepidness. An individuality. I bet he was the one who'd dug the holes in the fire-engine road.

He'd gone in through one entrance and popped what he probably thought was strategically out of another. I could imagine him telling the others he was just going to have a look-see, and them pleading with him to be careful. At length he withdrew into the sett again and the wood once more appeared deserted. Charles and I stirred from our watching posts, deciding that the show was over—only to disturb two more badgers who were up on the fire-engine road and who hurtled down it as if the spooks were after them.

This was the reason for all those holes along the verge. It was a favourite promenade of the badgers. In the weeks that followed, so long as Annabel was with us, we could pretty well guarantee to see some of them on it. A good surface to move on, nobody about at night—for them it was like the Grand Trunk Road in Kim. With plenty of escape holes to nip into if anyone *should* come along . . . if they couldn't go under it without people stuffing tree-trunks down their tunnels, use the road itself was obviously their motto.

Had we, in Annabel, stumbled on the perfect badger decoy? It rather seemed that we had. Though these, of course, probably wouldn't be very nervous badgers, living where nobody would normally harass them.

Years before there'd been an active sett very near the cottage—just down the Valley, in a wood on the side of the hill. Nobody had known much about that colony, either, except old Frank, who had a cabin in the wood. He was a bachelor and lived there on his own, working when he felt like it for a nearby farmer. The badgers often used to wake him up when they were fighting, he said—if it was moonlight he could see them going at it through the cabin window. He told us that he used to go out with a rolled-up newspaper and whack them on their bottoms to break up the fight. We didn't believe him, of course. Old Frank was noted for the tales he told when primed with the local cider. Now, after our own experience, we wondered. Do badgers who live where they have no cause to be afraid become more quickly used to the presence of humans? Or was it that they accepted old Frank as one of themselves—as, it seemed, they did Annabel?

After that we saw them unfailingly when we took her with us and rarely had much success when we didn't —except on the occasion when we took Louisa and my cousin Dee. We left Annabel at home then. The others had to get back to town that night and Annabel, except when she feels like galloping, always dawdles interminably on the track. Once more we took up watching positions—I behind my usual tree, Charles and Louisa and Dee up on the fire-engine road. They really should have come into the wood, I thought. It was silly standing up there in a row. Though probably we wouldn't see anything without Annabel to cover our scent. . . .

That was as much thought as I had time for. At that moment, within minutes of our taking up position, a badger came up out of a hole just in front of me, looked around for an instant and glided off into the wood. I glanced up to see if the others had seen it... they should have been in *here*, I remember telling myself... and then I noticed there was another badger out, heading straight towards them!

It was making—my heart sank as I realised it—right for Louisa. Louisa is my aunt, but is far too young for me to call her that. She is more like my elder sister—very game, but somewhat timid. She'd been enquiring all the way up as to whether badgers bite. Dee, on the other hand, has nerves of steel. I couldn't imagine her being nervous of a badger. One squall from Louisa, however, and the night's viewing would be over. I waited resignedly for it to come.

Then I saw the expression on her face. She was leaning forward enraptured, like someone looking at a particularly enchanting puppy. Scared of a badger biting her? If it came any nearer it looked as if Louisa would be picking it up and hugging it!

That eventuality being avoided by the badger realising something was afoot and nipping down a hole just before it got to her, the next item on the programme was the emergence, this time from the hole in front of me, of a family unit that I recognised. First the boar who'd nearly fallen over Charles—I knew him at once; there was no mistaking him. Then the smaller female, a yard or two behind him, and after her, popping out like furry Jack-in-the-boxes, the now familiar cubs. One cub, two, following in line behind their parents. ... Where, I wondered, was the third? A pause... a belated rush... and he was out too, tearing off to catch up with the others. Doing a Chaplinesque kick with his hind leg as he went, just for the fun of it. Obviously he was going to grow up like his father.

I watched them trek off, still in line, through the wood. I could hardly believe I was actually seeing it. I looked up at the fire-engine road. Louisa appeared to be in a trance. Dee nodded imperceptibly to signify that she'd seen them. There were more up on the road, too, a slight turn of her head indicated. Charles was standing there motionless; hawk-sighted; missing nothing.

The cubs were growing now. They were much bigger than when we'd first seen them. Instead of playing near the sett with them the parents were taking them out for the night. Off looking for food, down to the stream to drink—they wouldn't be back again for hours. We waited for a while, though. More adults came out and made off. Wherever we looked, it seemed, there were badgers.

Was it that the wind was particularly in our favour? Had the badgers grown used to us—even though this time we hadn't got Annabel? Was it that all four of us have a particularly strong animal rapprochement? Though so do other people, of course, and they still don't have this much luck with badgers.

We were there for about three-quarters of an hour before we decided they must all be out. In that time, we calculated later, between us we'd seen twelve. The others had seen a second female and two cubs on the fire-engine road and there were the adults who'd come out on their own.

We went home on air, scarcely able to believe this had happened to us. It was something few people ever see. Something we shall remember all our lives, thanks to Mio and Annabel.

Chapter Twelve

Life wasn't all riding and badger-watching, of course. There was always plenty to do at the cottage. Gardening, wine-making, Charles working among his fruit trees, on whose problems he had become quite an expert.

He had problems in plenty, what with the soil, the altitude and the fact that, high up though we might be, we were in a valley among the hills and therefore in a potential frost pocket. For that reason he'd moved all the pear trees from the bottom of the orchard to the top —pears being the earliest fruit trees to blossom and so most likely to be caught by the frost.

"Theest still 'on't grow 'em in this soil," Father Adams predicted happily. "Pears 'on't stand lime. It turns 'em yellow. And if that don't get 'em, then the mineral will." Trees do tend to die quite suddenly round here and the locals always say the roots have touched mineral.

"Han't ever bin no apples come to nuthin' in this village," Fred Ferry's uncle, old Sam Ferry, told us. There have been Ferrys in the district since before the Armada—a fact which, since someone researching local history unfortunately discovered it and even more unfortunately told Sam, has resulted in his acting as though he's been here since before the Armada himself and remembers everything that has happened personally.

I questioned him once about a handed-down story I'd heard about there having been Redshanks up at the camp—Redshanks being an old name for the Danes, who did a lot of invading round here.

"Oh ah, I remembers they all right. Th'old Squire had a herd on 'em," said Sam. Even when I explained they were Danes—men, not cows—he still insisted that he knew all about them. "Camped up there one summer and caught the hill afire," he said. He is probably right about that. Though I can't quite go along with his claim that he used to supply them with milk.

I was talking about Charles's determination to succeed with his fruit trees, however. He'd combatted the lime; overcome, he hoped, the frost problem; most of them were now draped in nets to stop the bullfinches getting at the buds. This worked well except on the occasions when a bird got inside the net. It then had a beanfeast on the buds while it waited, secure in the knowledge that when Charles, raise Cain about bullfinches though he might at other times, came along, he'd promptly cut a hole in the net to let it out.

He'd introduced bees to fertilise the fruit trees, too, but unfortunately had proved allergic to their stings. Untended, the bees had eventually swarmed and left us, much to my relief. I wasn't at all keen on them myself. What with the remembrance of Charles laid out cold on the kitchen floor with sixteen stings on his arms and knees and my eternally being afraid of Seeley poking one. But darn me if the following May a fresh swarm didn't take over the empty hive and we were right back where we started.

Charles was absolutely delighted—they made all the

difference to the fruit trees, he said. They worked diligently through the summer and, when the winter came, he insisted on feeding them to keep them going. I remember, once more making bee-candy, thinking I must be mad. All the trouble the first lot had caused. Seeley's propensity for poking things. But how can one deliberately let living creatures starve, even if they do sting the hand that feeds them?

They wouldn't get him this time, Charles assured me. He wouldn't open up the hive again. If I could make the candy so that it could be cut into strips, he'd just put a strip at a time in the entrance of the hive at dusk and leave them to work on it quietly.

A bright idea which I improved on. I set drinking straws in the tray of candy. About fifty of them, parallel, like the slats of a Venetian blind. Cut between those when the candy was set, I explained, and he'd have reinforced bars, the thickness of pencils, that would be simple to slip into the hive.

Charles, agreeing it was ingenious, inspected the tray. "You've plugged the ends of the straws, have you?" he asked. When I asked what on earth for . . . "So that the bees won't put their heads in them and not be able to get out," said Charles. "One always has to think of these things in advance."

Not to the extent of plugging the ends of fifty drinking straws I hadn't. Those bees had to take their chance. I had to admire their industry, however, when Charles brought back the straws they'd finished with. Clean as a whistle, not a sign of stickiness anywhere, every grain of candy carefully removed and stored. Ready to feed the young bees—and now, as a result, we had a tremendously active hive.

By gosh, they'd done wonders for the blackcurrants and gooseberries, said Charles. And the apple crop was going to be terrific. The plums were always pretty good; plums grow well around here. Even they looked like excelling themselves, however, what with the good weather and the bees.

It meant a lot of work, of course. Spraying, watering, feeding, keeping an eye on the birds. Meantime one of the garage doors fell off—it had been dragging on its hinges for years. The side gate was pretty shaky, too, and Charles was putting up a second conservatory.

Which was why, one morning, I came to be sweeping the cottage chimney. It was summer, and a fine one, but the sun goes early in the Valley and the evenings can be cool in our thick-walled cottage. We like a fire to stretch our legs by, and so do the cats, but the previous night it had started smoking. The sweep, when I rang up, was on holiday. It was the obvious time for him to *be* away. Not many people want their chimneys swept in the middle of July. Only us, and we didn't want to wait a fortnight, so we decided to do it ourselves.

I could do it on my own in fact, I said, as Charles had so many other jobs on hand. We had a set of rods—most people have in the country; they are used for drains as well as chimneys. And it wouldn't take very long. About an hour I reckoned, after which I'd do the laundry. It was nice to think that in emergencies we were so self-contained.

It *shouldn't* have taken long. It consists, after all, only of screwing rods together, fixing a brush on the end of them and pushing them up the chimney till the brush goes out through the pot. I'd watched the sweep do it many a time. You had to take particular care to clean the pot out when you burn wood, he'd told me once. Wood-smoke cakes it more solidly than anything.

So there I was, heaving up and down on the rods, a

scarf over my hair, a dust-sheet over the fireplace. I'd

checked the brush was out through the pot. When I looked it was sticking out like a sunflower with two children on ponies out in the lane regarding it with interest. Remote we may be, in our tucked-away valley, but whatever we do we can always be sure of an audience.

I'd gone indoors, pulled it back a rod-length and, remembering what the sweep had said, was working it industriously up and down in the pot itself when Charles came in from repairing the garage door to see how I was getting on. "Fine," I said. "I've done it really thoroughly. I'll just give one more push for luck."

Which I did, started to withdraw the rods, and unfortunately they came down without the brush. It hadn't fallen off in the chimney, either, where I might have easily dislodged it. It was—my heart sank when I put the rods up again to investigate—sitting like a bird in a cage in the chimney pot, and there was only one way to get it out.

For the next hour or so we could be seen—and were seen—by the never ending posses of more small children on ponies who kept going past the back gate (there was a junior pony club rally on apparently; I couldn't have picked a better day to get the brush stuck).... We could be seen, as I say, carrying ladders round to the back of the cottage, heaving them up and across the tiles, tethering Annabel so she couldn't, as is her wont with ladders, playfully push them down again—and finally Charles climbing up, hanging on to the chimney pot with one hand, and plunging a stick up and down it with the other.

It worked. The brush came down. There was still plenty to interest our young audience, however, who seemed to be engaged in some sort of relay race in which they kept dashing past the cottage in groups in one direction and appearing ten minutes later from the other. For a start there was Charles descending from the roof with an intriguingly black face and carrying the ladders away, which understandably upset some of the ponies. And still the show wasn't over. There was a further instalment to come.

Having cleaned up the mess I turned on the washing machine, did the laundry and then switched on the pump to pump out the water. Thinking vengefully of the time I'd wasted on account of the brush getting stuck, it was some while before I noticed that no water was going down the sink. It was flooding gently, like an autumn tide in St. Mark's Square in Venice, all over the kitchen floor. A pipe had split inside the machine.

Brace up. Don't give way, I remember telling myself. Nothing will be gained by hitting it. I wheeled the machine to the door and switched on again, calmly, so that it could pump itself out into the yard. Which was why the members of the pony club—none of whom I recognised as being local and they'd probably decided by this time that whoever lived in our cottage must be mad—came past on their next circuit to the rivetting spectacle of me sweeping gallons of water out through the kitchen door while the washing machine gushed further gallons out past the fishpool.

At least it didn't go into the fishpool, which has a retaining wall around it, and eventually order was restored and we had a belated lunch. We'd better be careful though, I said. Things always went in threes. I was very relieved when, that evening, Seeley broke a drinking glass.

Which just shows how wrong one can be. Not long before we'd had the bathroom altered at the cottage and this had involved the construction, in one place, of a new cavity wall with a window in it. A builder had done the main work but Charles had opted to do the finishing touches himself—put in the window sills, for instance, build an airing-cupboard, alter an adjacent door.

He did a spell on the airing-cupboard one day; a session on the window-sill another. I'd be amazed, he was always telling me, how all these projects would eventually arrive at culmination.

The morning after the affair of the chimney pot and the washing machine, he got up, did a bit to the door before breakfast, put the hammer on the window space while he got himself a nail, and the hammer, obviously to spite him, fell down inside the cavity. A good six feet down, where whatever he did he couldn't reach it. His *best* hammer, said Charles, appearing in the kitchen to tell me about it. Now *that* was going to hold things up.

It did. It was two days before we hit on the idea of putting glue on the end of the broom-handle, balancing the broom-handle on the hammer and leaving it to set overnight. It worked. Up came the hammer next morning. It was a wonderful advertisement for the glue. It was pretty resourceful of us, too, we thought. We were very pleased with ourselves. The neighbour who came in to borrow a ladder, though, and found us gazing proudly at a hammer stuck to a broom-handle.... He agreed it was a good idea when we explained it to him. But he gave us a rather old-fashioned look.

I've no doubt that one went round the village. Things like that spread like wildfire in the country. Like the tales that kept filtering down to us of the doings of the chatelaine of the Tower House. I hadn't seen her for quite a while. I'd heard she still went out with two horses. But she wasn't bringing them through the Valley now. She was concentrating in the opposite direction. Intent, according to those who observe these things, on getting to know people who mattered.

Having obviously decided that nobody in our village did, she was now patronising a neighbouring community—and, according to the reports, not succeeding very well there either. She'd joined one organisation whose chairman, the wife of a retired Colonel, knew everybody for miles around. Just the one for our heroine to cultivate and she assiduously went about doing it, to the extent that when the Colonel's wife announced there was going to be a summer fête and asked for volunteers to make cakes for the cake stall, the woman from the Tower House said that she would provide the lot.

That didn't go down well for a start. Making cakes for fêtes is a matter of public prestige. No organisation member is going to be done out of that. She'd eventually been restrained to giving four, apparently, and the day of the fête arrived, and there were the stalls draped with flags on the Colonel's lawn and the ladies in charge of them in little aprons, importantly receiving supplies.

The woman from the Tower House, however, brooked no dealing with underlings. She took her cakes up to the house, to present them to the Chairman personally. Mrs. Benton perhaps *should* have been supervising the fête preparations, but she always was a law unto herself. So far as she was concerned the bunfight wasn't till the afternoon, and she had minions to deal with the details. She came round from the back when the bell rang, her arms dripping with soapsuds, wearing an old raincoat with the sleeves rolled up and her husband's deerstalker on her head. She fixed the intruder with the sort of look for which Colonel's wives are renowned. "I'm washing m'dog. I'll deal with you later," she said, sailing back round the corner to where her terrier waited in its bath.

"As if I were a Nobody," the woman from the Tower House later told somebody she knew. Who in due course, villages being what they are, told somebody else, who told us.

Chapter Thirteen

Actually I felt rather sorry for her. She seemed to like country life and if it weren't for this silly superiority business she might have fitted in very well. I felt even more sorry when I heard what happened next, though I have to admit that I laughed.

She had, it seemed, joined the Women's Institute—in this other village, not ours. Ern Biggs's sister was a member and the story came back via him. The Colonel's wife was chairman of that too, as often happens in small communities, and our heroine, still in pursuit in spite of her setback over the cakes, was now busily being a member.

Most democratically, by all accounts. "Sat next to our Lil," Ern recounted. "Shared her spoon to stir her tea with. Lil said she couldn't half sing Jerusalem." All of which recommendations unfortunately went straight down the drain when she won the monthly competition, the prize for which was an ox-tongue, given by the local butcher.

" 'N' she ixcepted it," said Ern, telling me the story when he met me in the lane. "Took it home, had it cooked, and they *et* it!"

"What was wrong with that?" I asked. I'd have done the same myself. She'd probably felt so democratic doing it, too. I wouldn't have known—and she hadn't known either, that being her very first meeting—that what she was expected to do was to re-donate it as the next month's prize, whereupon it went back into store in the butcher's freezer. Presumably to show how they valued it. This was the third time it had come out.

Personally I escaped such involvements. Writing, looking after the cottage and Charles and the animals, going up to see the badgers... these took up all my time. And trying to improve my riding of Mio, of course; a goal I pursued with ever-hopeful application.

It was around this time that I met up with Tina, who was a nurse at a local hospital. She was small, a tomboy and game for anything, which was why she rode Cobnut, who was also small and full of zip. He was a little dark chestnut gelding. The Hutchings hadn't had him very long. Long enough, however, to discover that he had a sensitive mouth which could be damaged by too much pulling on it, so they'd fitted him with a rubber bit—which made things rather complicated seeing that his other characteristic was to go like the wind.

That was how, looking over my shoulder one day to see who it was coming up behind us with an unfamiliarly short, staccato drumming of hooves... not the deceptively languid-sounding beat of Zab's canter that could take him past us like a bird if he wanted; not the furious, charging clatter that meant Merlin was feeling good this morning and out of the way everybody, here he came.... I first saw Tina on him, coming past the others like the Pony Express.

The Apaches would never have caught her. I've never seen a pony's legs go so fast. Up and down like a sewing machine, neck out, mane flying, leaning at a tautly professional angle as he came round the horseshoe bend, with Tina, a look of joy on her face, encouraging him to "Come on, Nutty." Excusing herself later that it was difficult to hold him, with only that rubber bit.

He came to mean to her what Mio meant to me and after that we often raced each other. For Mio he took the place of Iggy—somebody with whom he could have fun. Zab was too aloof; too superior. Now Mio had another friend.

Being friends, apart from nipping each other on the bottom whenever possible, like a couple of children playing Touch, consisted of getting together at the front of the ride ready for the signal to canter, prancing along sideways, each trying to set the other off and, when one of them succeeded, both of them using it as an excuse to go.

It was just as well we were in front on those occasions. We'd have stampeded the others like sheep if we weren't. "Now *walk* up here," Mrs. Hutchings would patiently instruct us. "Hold them till you get to the top. Make them trot a few yards first. Don't let them go until you're ready."

It was all very well to talk, but if Mio walked, Nutty would start dancing about behind him. "Look out! He's coming!" Mio would snort and, airborne, we'd be gone. Or Nutty, walking for once as demurely as a choirboy in procession, would see Mio start capering about in front of him and I, fighting to keep Mio's head down, would hear Tina screech "Nutty!" in the rear.

I gave up and let him go then. It was either that or be nearly knocked off by the rush of wind as Nutty belted past. In which case Mio did his Pegasus leap and belted after him, and the result was the same in the end.

We enjoyed it, of course, but it wasn't the way to

ride, with the horses doing just as they liked. Once we went round a bend like rockets and met the Forestry Landrover coming in the other direction. The Forestry manager always drove slowly and the horses did pull up, but we should have been trotting round there. And then there was the time I frightened Miss Adkin's horse and blotted my copybook for weeks.

Miss Adkin was a rider of the old school. Rode to hounds, knew horses backwards, practically lived in the saddle. She looked down on people who hired horses from stables. "Amateurs" she described them loftily. Which was why, when we met her, we automatically straightened ourselves and rode as well as we could. Which was why, too, the morning we were climbing up a steep path in the Forest preparatory to turning off along a cantering track to the right, and there she was coming downhill in the opposite direction, I was determined to do everything just so.

I was ahead of everybody else. Even Tina was behind for once. Mrs. Hutchings, ever hopeful, had sent me on with instructions to just *try* to walk the first few yards along the cantering track before I let Mio take off. If everybody else stayed back, she said, particularly Tina, so that Mio couldn't hear anyone at his heels . . . and if I remembered to sit down *hard* the moment he started dancing . . . we never knew, with a bit of luck, one of these days I might manage it.

So there we were. Miss Adkin and I advancing towards each other like a pair of duellists on Hampstead Heath at dawn. She on a great grey hunter with a couple of dogs at her heels, I in due course turning off to the right a few yards ahead of her, praying hard that Mio would behave.

He didn't, of course. Two steps round the corner on one of his favourite galloping tracks and Mio began to toss his head. Any moment now he'd start prancing sideways and she'd see I couldn't control him. Better, I thought, to look as if I intended to gallop, rather than end up round his neck. So we went—and, the others told me later, so did Miss Adkin on her horse, flat out in the other direction.

It was reaction, of course. The business of one horse going when another does, and, being a competent rider, she stopped him before he got very far. It isn't done, however—and can be very dangerous—to startle another rider's mount. For weeks after that, when I saw her riding past the cottage, I hid behind the coalhouse door.

After this Mrs. Hutchings suggested that perhaps special concentration might help, so for a while Tina and I rode with her alone. One of us deliberately tearing off in front while the other did her best to hold back, or side by side, alternating ten beats full out with ten in close controlled canter. We capered across the hill-tracks, too, mentally singing the Skater's Waltz, regulating the horse's canter to the lusty, swaying rhythm. Tina got carried away one day and sang it aloud by mistake, and Cobnut, astonished, stopped dead in his tracks to listen.

We improved, though—or the horses did—and Mrs. Hutchings suggested we went out on our own. There was no point in our being hampered by the others, she said. We ought to be able to manage them now. "Practise that ten full out, ten controlled beat," she told us. "It'll give you tremendous confidence."

It did. We practised that, had a couple of chases along

the cantering tracks, all the time in full control. It had been worth putting in all that work, I said, to know I could stop Mio now just when I liked.

We were, at that moment, walking them towards the gate leading to the Downs, about a quarter of a mile ahead. Tina said later that when, the next instant, I was gone, she thought I'd done it deliberately. To show her what control and confidence I had, though she wondered why I hadn't told her I was going. Always game for a race, however, she took off after me, expecting me to rein to a halt where the track divided, near its end. "And then you went straight on," she said, "and I thought 'My gosh! She's going to jump the gate!'"

So did I. I nearly fell off with sheer relief when Mio stopped as he'd done before and began to crop the verge. Hadn't had fun like that for ages, had we? he snorted, tugging zestfully at a clump of dandelions. He bet I was as fed up as he was with this ten quick, ten slow business.

So there I was, obviously as much under his hoof as I'd ever been. One day though, I told him, I'd succeed. So I practised on, and cooked and gardened and talked to passers-by which was how I came to learn some more interesting facts about horses.

You wouldn't have thought him a horsy type—a big bald man with an expensive car which was parked by the side of the ford. He was sitting in it with his wife, the window down, watching the bees fetching water. When he saw Charles and me he got out and came over to the wall, asking was that our hive up in the orchard?

He didn't look like a beekeeper either, but it seemed that he had been in former years. He had us entranced with his stories about them. The swarms he'd taken, the stings he'd had—ten to every spoonful of honey, he reckoned. And how he'd once bested a gypsy who'd thought to have the laugh on him and his neighbour.

Our passer-by was a retired Cornish farmer, and of course nearly everybody in Cornwall grows violets, and one day his neighbour, going along a country lane in a bus, saw a roadside advertisement for violet plants, which were being offered very cheaply. He thought he'd like to go there and get some, but he didn't have a car, so he asked the farmer, who took him over in his truck, which turned out to be just as well.

The place where they were for sale was on the edge of a wood, said our friend, and the proprietor was a gypsy. Nothing wrong with that, of course, but he wasn't very accommodating in his manner. His neighbour said he wanted a thousand plants and asked how much they'd be. "You can have them for nothing if you like to dig them out yourself," said the gypsy. "I haven't got time to do it."

They did wonder about that, said our friend . . . putting up a For Sale notice and then offering to give them away free. . . . But the gypsy'd walked away and there was the violet bed in front of them. Very good plants by the look of it, and if the gypsy didn't want them. . . .

They were large plants. Each would divide into ten. They only needed to dig a hundred. The neighbour picked up a spade and advanced towards the bed and the farmer went to the truck to get some sacks. And then he heard his neighbour yell and turned to see him drop his spade and start running.

There were bees, he said, coming out of those woods like thunderclouds and his neighbour was going as if he had a bull behind him. And the gypsy had come back with a bee-veil on and was laughing his head off at the spectacle.

"He said," said our friend, "that he had forty hives inside the wood and when the bees were working you couldn't go near the plants. That was when he chalked up the advertisement, just for a joke, for the fun of seeing people get chased." Nobody'd ever got a single plant yet, the gypsy boasted.

"No?" said our friend. "Then just watch this." Before the gypsy's astonished eyes he picked up the spade, went over and dug up the hundred plants. Slowly, methodically, unhurriedly, being used to dealing with bees. "Free, I think you said," he commented, loading them into the truck. Apparently the gypsy was mad as a hatter. They never saw the sign again.

He had dozens of stories about bees. How we got round to horses I can't recall. I remember various tales about the farm cats, and the cow that suffered with nerves.

It seemed that he went one day with his cousin, who was an agricultural college-trained expert, to buy four Red Devon cows. Three they agreed on. The fourth, a beautiful animal with a fine set of horns, his cousin didn't like. It was neurotic, he said; he could tell; it would be more trouble than a whole herd of normal cows put together. Anybody'd spend more time being kicked out of the cowhouse by that one than he'd spend inside doing the milking. Our friend liked the look of it, however, so he bought it.

"Surprising what they teach 'em at these colleges," he said. When they got home that cow fought so hard while they were unloading it they thought it would strangle itself on the rope. For days they kept it hobbled in the cow-house, where it refused to eat or drink and kicked everybody and everything that passed it. Every time our friend went by he offered it cow-nuts and spoke to it but all the cow did was try to kick him. Eventually, with patience, he did tame it; he got it eating from his hand and it would follow him wherever he went. It never lost its nervousness of other people, however. If he was taking the cows along the lane and someone came the other way, he would hold up the skirt of his milking coat and the cow would put her head underneath and he'd take her past like that.

She turned out a wonderful milker though, said our friend. He was never sorry he'd bought her. I nodded, entranced by the thought of that cow with its head under his milking coat. "And she was a beautiful creature. She had a fine set of horns," he said.

Loving animals as he did, and admiring beauty and strength in them, it was not surprising that when the Second World War broke out and some of the Bertram Mills circus horses were being sold, he should buy a Suffolk Punch called Snowy—a bareback riding horse with the mark on his back where, over the years, the riders' feet had landed. He was surprised, he said, that a bareback pony could be so broad; they didn't look like that when they were in the ring. He'd commented on this and the seller had told him that the horses were French-chalked and shaded—made up, in fact, so that their backs looked much narrower under the arc-lights, but actually they were so broad that anybody jumping through the hoop just couldn't miss. I could think of somebody who would, I thought, imagining myself up there trying to do it. But I didn't interrupt. This was somebody who knew animals. I could have listened to him talking for hours.

We pretty well did. How his young daughter used to ride Snowy poised on one foot like a ballet dancer, while the great horse, showing his paces, circled proudly round the yard. How someone he knew confirmed Snowy's age—he was said to be around eight years old when he bought him.

"He asked me to exercise him a bit," he said, "and then, when he was hot, this man wetted his finger, drew it down Snowy's brow, and counted the horizontal wrinkles. An old gypsy had given him that tip. One wrinkle a year . . . an odd bit for less than a year. I hadn't told him how old Snowy was supposed to be. He reckoned seven and three-quarters."

Snowy the clever one, Snowy the powerful . . . he'd obviously worshipped that horse. "And he was so gentle," he said, launching off into another story. This time about one of the farm kittens who was a particular friend of Snowy's.

He had double electric fences around his fields when the cows were in them, he told us—the top one to keep the cows in, the bottom one to stop the calves from getting underneath. There were always one or two cats accompanying him when he went to see the cows, and one day he and his wife were going through the field with the kitten romping beside them. . . . They never bothered to turn off the electricity; he always jumped the fence and his wife crawled underneath; and while she was doing it on this occasion and he was standing by, to see she got well down and under, the kitten stood on its hind legs and, before anybody could stop it, touched its nose inquisitively to the wire.

He actually saw sparks coming out of its nose . . . cats take in twice the electricity that we do . . . and then it took off, understandably like lightning, and they ran after it to see if it was all right. They found it with Snowy who, with his legs straddled carefully apart, could be seen looking down at something between his forefeet in his field. There was the kitten, rolling about, rubbing its nose with its paws, mewing so indignantly it was obviously telling him the story. And, from the expression on his face, Snowy was sympathetically listening to it.

Years later, when they'd sold the farm, their main concern was where Snowy would go. They were moving to a bungalow, with no room for a Suffolk Punch. Very reluctantly they advertised him. One prospective buyer, however, turned out to be the farmer's schoolfriend, and he bought him for his grandsons and never parted with him again. "I never missed a week without going to see him," said the farmer. "He was well over twenty when he died."

He stood silently for a moment, remembering the old horse, then brightened again as he thought of another story. How the friend who bought him, when he came to look at him, opened his mouth, looked knowledgeably inside and nodded. "Tell me," said the farmer, "what *do* people go by when they look inside a horse's mouth? I've always wondered but never liked to ask."

"I don't know either," his friend said equably. "But I know it's the right thing to do."

Chapter Fourteen

When, during the course of conversation, I mentioned my own experiences with Mio, the man from Cornwall said that horses knew more than people imagined.

How this applied in my case I wasn't quite sure. Whether Mio knew intuitively that I liked to go (he was right there of course, so long as it was in the proper place and at the proper time); whether he knew that if he took off he'd frighten the daylights out of me (he was right there too; even while I was enjoying the speed I was wondering where and how I was going to stop him); whether it was, as Mrs. Hutchings said she'd decided, that I had an electric bottom... she found herself lying awake at night, she said, trying to think of some technique that would work, but short of putting an anchor on Mio she hadn't yet come up with one ... he also knew that I was never cross with him; that in the end I'd pat his neck and say he was super and hadn't it been fun, and he'd high-step it jauntily back to the stables, no doubt telling the others that I was Improving.

That animals do reason more deeply than people think we knew from our own experience... with Blondin, the squirrel who'd once lived with us, with our Siamese cats, and, when it came to the horse family, with Annabel. One thing she'd done over the badger-watching business had certainly shown considerable reasoning. She hadn't stirred an inch when the badgers appeared that first night we took her up, just glanced at them and gone on eating. Raising her head when she'd got a mouthful of grass and watching them speculatively while she chewed... as she might look at a flock of sheep; certainly not with concern. She'd walked placidly home with us afterwards along the night-darkened Forestry paths, her small hooves pattering confidently.... Was she thinking, we asked her, of her bed?

What must have been computerizing in her mind was our interest in those badgers. We'd gone all that way to look at them. Watched them as if they mattered. Supposing those little ones followed us back to the cottage—she bet we'd take them in. Have them indoors with us probably, like we did those cats, while she had to stand on the hillside and watch what went on through the window....

That, at any rate, is the only explanation we can give for the fact that as soon as we got back, legs sturdily straddled, she deliberately spent a penny in the yard. Right outside the kitchen door where we had to step over it to get in. Normally she did it by her field gate, or inside the door of her stable. Annabel's mark, on her territory, warning other animals to Keep Out. Now she was putting her mark on the cottage, to show that that was her preserve. Wasn't having any badgers over *that* doorstep, said the sway of her bottom, as she pattered complacently towards her stable.

Not long ago someone put forward the theory that horses can "tap" the human mind. Discussing this, Lynn said that Gusto particularly seemed able to read her thoughts. She'd be giving a lesson in the field, she said, with Gusto doing the same thing for several rounds, and time and again she'd open her mouth to give another order—to change direction, perhaps, or canter instead of trot—and before she could say a word, Gusto was already doing what she wanted. Sometimes she found herself wondering if she was going bonkers—if perhaps she *had* already said it aloud.

Snowy's owner had poured out instances of his intelligence like sand running through an hourglass. How you could tell him, from three or four fields away, to go home to Missus and that horse would start out on his own. How you could call after him to come back again and halfway there though he might be, Snowy would turn in the lane and obediently plod back. How he considered himself the guardian of the cows when he was with them and if anyone left the gate open he'd herd them into a corner of the field and patrol between them and the gate, whinnying till somebody came and fastened them in.

He was a circus horse born and bred. For him to work out the principles of cattle-herding was really quite remarkable. If he'd watched the farm dog doing it and was copying him, it was still extremely intelligent. A Suffolk Punch herding cattle would have been something on a Western ranch. As, no doubt, when it came about, was the sight of us herding them ourselves.

We'd always intended to visit Canada. Charles, which is why he is fond of the open spaces, was himself born in Montreal and lived as a small boy in New Brunswick. He'd come back to England with his parents when he was still quite young but he remembered a lot about it. Snow up to the top of the porch-roof in winter.

Going on fishing trips with his father. Eating trout cooked over a camp-fire on the river-bank and seeing

bears ambling through the woods. And, once, doing a train trip with his parents right across Canada to see his uncle and aunt in Vancouver. He could still hear the haunting whistle, he said, as the train went through the Rockies. One day we'd go back there. When we could spare the time.

That, what with the fruit trees and all the jobs to be done about the place and the fact that Sheba was now very old, appeared to be still in the distant future when one day Dee rang up. She was in a state of considerable agitation. Cousin Ben, she said, was coming over.

It so happened that I, too, had relatives in Canada, though I knew very little about them. One of my grandmother's brothers had gone out there some sixty years before and founded another branch of the family. He'd had two sons, who in turn had had children, and one of them was a clergyman. All I knew about them other than that was a dramatic account of my grandmother's about their log cabin having burnt down. Not long after they got there, she said. All they'd saved was a side of bacon.

My grandmother didn't have much time for letter-writing, what with her own large family to bring up and keeping the neighbours in order, but Dee's father, who was another of her brothers, had corresponded regularly with Canada. After he died Dee kept up the correspondence with her Canadian uncle's widow, Aunt Ellen. It was Aunt Ellen who'd written now, to say that Ben was coming over. Ben was the clergyman, a Rural Dean, and he was coming for an ecclesiastical conference. At the end of which, said, Aunt Ellen, he'd like to stay with Dee for a while and get to know some of the family.

"What's wrong with that?" I asked. Dee being one of the most hospitable people on earth, I couldn't think what she was worrying about.

"A *clergyman*!" wailed Dee.... "All that home-made wine I've made. What'll he *think* when he sees the cupboards full of bottles? And my language.... I don't mind a damn slipping out, but suppose I should say anything worse...."

She hid the home-made wine, but it didn't matter. Cousin Ben preferred whisky anyway. We never saw a dog-collar. He wore jeans and a yellow zip-up jacket. And when he flew back, complete with a whole Cheddar cheese from Cheddar, and reported on his English relations, within months his uncle and aunt came over ... the Entente Cordiale had started.

They invited us back to Canada, and Dee went first. She had a wow of a time. With us, though, Sheba was ailing—she was now sixteen and a half. We felt we couldn't cross the Atlantic and leave her. Supposing she died while we were away? We wanted to be with her at the end. She died, in fact, while Dee was in Canada. We buried her with Solomon. The following summer we left Seeley at Low Knap with his new sister, Shebalu, and Annabel went to the farm . . . she'd gone up there since we first had her; she loved it with the cows. And now I felt like pinching myself; I couldn't believe it was true; Charles and I, in Canada at last, were driving down the road from Edmonton. In what Leonard, Ben's uncle, termed his automobile, with our luggage in what he called the trunk. "You folk all right?" he said putting his foot to the accelerator. "We shan't be very long."

We weren't. We were going about three hundred miles south as the crow flies, first of all to Ben's, then on to the ranch of a friend of his in the foothills of the Rockies. "Where I thought you'd like to stay for a while," said Ben, "for the atmosphere and the horses."

We added another hundred miles to that by way of a

detour to see the Alberta Badlands. We stopped at restaurants a couple of times to eat, and several times to look at the view . . . the endless yellow sea of the wheat prairies, with the jagged purple outline of the Rockies beyond them. And still it was only just dark as we turned off from the main highway, along the gravel road that led out through the hills to the ranch.

For me it had already been a day of surprises. First the heat of the sun and the flatness of the landscape, that so much reminded me of the Camargue. And then I'd seen something that really shook me. Men wearing cowboy hats. I'd thought those belonged to the old days of the West—that people only wore them now in films or on television. But lorries (I beg their pardon; *trucks*) kept passing us with stetson-hatted drivers at the wheel. Men lounged at store doors and filling stations as we passed, looking like characters out of The Virginian.

"What did you expect them to wear?" Leonard's wife, Nellie, enquired. Well . . . but I hadn't known the West was still as real as this.

I hadn't seen anything yet. Later, while we were having a quick lunch at a roadside restaurant . . . hamburgers, French fries and salad, with maple ice-cream and coffee to follow . . . a group of men trooped in and sat at a table. All of them, without exception, wore checked shirts, Huckleberry Finn braces, wide black hats and Biblical beards. Some of them were in their twenties but they still looked like Old Testament prophets. "Hutterites," whispered Nellie, seeing my surreptitious stare.

They are a German-speaking sect that live together in agricultural colonies, refuse to fight or pay taxes and are entirely self-supporting. They live and dress like the early pioneers. The men wear these broad-brimmed black hats and stop shaving when they marry. The women wear tight bodices, ankle-length dresses and cotton headscarves. The children, from the tiniest tots upwards, are dressed as miniature replicas of their parents. There were no women or children with the group in the restaurant. The sexes, said Nellie, eat and work as separate units. Obviously they get together sometimes, though. They have a considerable number of children.

I almost expected to see a covered wagon outside the restaurant when we left, but they'd come in an old Ford truck. There are lots of them in Western Canada—but what a stir they'd cause in England!

On we sped, skirting Calgary with its famous Husky Tower rising like a minaret above it and its brewery and spreading suburban houses. That could be anywhere, I thought, a little disappointed—and then I noticed the signs on posts along the road. Blackfoot Trail read the first ones. Later we took the Macleod Trail.

Sure, said Leonard, when I questioned him. The first highway followed the route of the old Blackfoot Indian trail south towards the Montana border. There were unpaved side bits in certain sections where you could still see the marks of their travois—the litters made of branches, with two pine poles as shafts, which dragged behind the horses, their back ends trailing on the ground. By this means they transported their teepees, and their children and their old people, on the annual migration as they followed the buffalo south. The travois poles had worn grooves in the trail which were still visible a hundred years later.

The second trail, he said, marked the line of the old trading route from Edmonton to Fort Macleod. They'd have come this way in the old days with dog teams, or with pack-horses in the summer....

He didn't need to tell me more. In my imagination they were there travelling with me. Seeing the same views over the prairies. Turning the same bends in the road. The women in sunbonnets; the canopied, two-wheeled Red River carts that had carried so many of them westwards ... made entirely of wood, even down to the ingeniously interlocked wheel-rims, so that they could be taken apart to cross rivers or repaired without the help of a blacksmith. The men with guns on their shoulders. The patient, plodding horses. In winter, the trappers coming down from the North, their sledges piled high with furs.

It was hard to imagine the Canadian winter now, though, with the roadside yellow with wheat, and prairie hawks sitting like lines of chessmen on the tele-

graph poles, scanning the landscape for prey. The poles are in such demand as look-out posts because there are no trees on the prairies ... except where there is water, along the streams and rivers ... and the hawks catch one's eye because the poles are so short, only about half the height of ours, with the thick single telegraph line hanging in scallops, so that it won't be broken by the weight of the snow.

We went through the little, isolated prairie towns . . . Nanton . . . Stavely . . . each with its cluster of tall, brightly-coloured grain elevators that are typical of Alberta. The towns, like the highway, follow the line of the old Canadian-Pacific railway—now, in the day of the automobile, mostly given over to freight. But the trains still have the mournful, haunting whistle that Charles remembered as a child. Funny, he said . . . it all seemed so strange . . . to think that, long ago, he had come through here. . . .

But now, with darkness falling, we were leaving the highway and the prairies, turning along a rough, gravelled road that led out into the hills. Soon the moon rose and silvered the landscape. It was a wonderful way to come upon the Western range for the first time. An area as vast and lonely as the prairies but consisting now, instead of flat land, of low-rolling hills and shadowy valleys that reminded me of pictures of the moon and looked equally remote.

My cousin stopped the car and opened the window. Hot as the day had been, the night struck cold as a mountain stream. "Straight off the Rockies," said Nellie. "From here they're only twenty miles away."

We sat there for a while looking round us and listening to the miles of silence. England and the Valley seemed part of another world. It was then that something slipped from behind a clump of bushes on to the trail ahead of us, looked at us for a moment and was gone. I had just time to see that it resembled a shortish grey Alsatian—with a greater breadth between its ears, though; more like a Husky dog's. "Coyote," said my cousin laconically. As in England we would say,

"A rabbit." And then I knew I was really in the West.

Chapter Fifteen

That evening, from the ranch verandah, we heard the coyotes calling in the hills. Prepared for it though we were, the eeriness of the screams sent a shiver up my spine. "Two of them," Sherm, our host, informed us, pausing over his coffee cup to listen. When I asked anxiously whether one of them might be caught in a trap—from the pitch of some of the screams it sounded as if that particular performer was in agony—he laughed. "Probably discussing the night's mouse-hunting," he said. "We don't kill coyotes on this ranch."

It was true. He and his wife Claire are keen conservationists—two of the many Canadians who have come to believe, in a land where for so long animals have been shot on sight, that protecting wildlife is not just sentiment but practical commonsense. He was serious about the coyotes' conversation, too. It has been proved that wolves, when they are howling, are conveying news to each other—the location of the caribou herds or of other wolves; even, in instances which have been actually verified, the passage of human beings through their territory. Why then shouldn't coyotes, who are cousins of the wolves, exchange similar information about mice? Mice or gophers, said Sherm, those being their principal diet. And since mice and gophers do a lot of damage to the crops, allowing the coyotes full range to hunt them ensures the proper balance of nature.

Full range on the SN ranch meant exactly that. The previous week, Sherm told us, they'd looked out of the ranch window in the moonlight and seen a coyote mooching around in the yard. Into the woodpile and out again, a sniff along the front of the barn, round the back of the horse trough . . . it was obviously searching for something. In the old days it would have been shot on sight on the presumption that it had come to raid the hen-run. In the old days the presumption would probably have been right; coyotes are very partial to chickens. But few people keep chickens on cattle ranches nowadays, beef-rearing being a large-scale, stream-lined business. Eggs are bought from such places as the Hutterite colonies, or from the supermarket in town. Unless they keep a special milking cow, even the milk is tinned.

So Sherm and Claire had watched to see what the coyote was after and it had eventually gone off with their young dog's ball. "Would it eat *that*?" I enquired, feeling sorry for it, thinking how hungry it must have been. "Oh no—it wanted it to play with," said Sherm. "Coyotes have a tremendous sense of fun." When I asked how they could have been sure it *was* a ball, in a coyote's mouth at night, Claire said they could see it easily; it was a large one, the size of a football.

The mind boggles at the picture that conjures up. A coyote trotting off with a playball, carrying it back to its den . . . and then sitting with it triumphantly outside the entrance and broadcasting to its neighbours about that!

This is a book about horses, however. I mustn't go on about coyotes. They, and the wolves and the bears, must wait for another time. But a coyote wanting a ball to play with, a wolf exchanging news with its friends, a she-bear smacking a cub's bottom for disobedience like a human mother, or glissading on her own rear down a slope through the snow for fun . . . hearing these things told of by people who had witnessed them, I felt that the West was my second home. I was even more sure of it next morning when I saw the horses in the corral.

I hadn't really considered how they get around on the range nowadays. In Land-rovers and trucks, I suppose I would have said. Keeping a horse or two for pleasure . . . and we'd heard that many of the ranchers had private planes. Sherm himself had a small two-seater that he used for nipping up to Calgary and for checking on the cattle. He often swept in low over the valley at dusk, navigation lights flashing on his wing-tips like outsize stars, coming down to land on the little strip behind the hayfield and then home in the truck to supper.

But the horses are not there as part of the decor. They are still vitally essential on the range, able to climb hills and slide down gullies or negotiate tracks where no vehicle could go. It can be miles by gravel road through one valley and back along another, and a matter of minutes on horseback over a hill. As for the intelligence of the Western cowpony, they told us—that had to be seen to be believed.

I'd heard about that, but I hardly expected to be introduced to a cowpony called Sheba. "Very intelligent, this one," said Sherm. "We thought you would like to ride her."

I looked at her and she looked at me. We each knew what the other was thinking. With that name, I thought, I hadn't a chance. I could forecast her temperament already. Wilful, determined ... I bet she was fast. There was a businesslike look about her. And she was obviously, complacently, mind-reading my qualms and filing them away for future reference.

"She's part Arab," said Sherm. There was no mistaking that. The head, the intelligent eyes, the slender legs. Nothing like Mio; she had a stomach like a barrel; but that obviously was by personal design. So that she wouldn't faint from lack of sustenance when she was running after the cattle—and to ensure that her saddle would slip. When we went out Charles rode Sherm's saddle horse, a big strawberry roan, as immoveably as a Texas Ranger. Try as I might, I rode the range persistently lopsided.

It was this business of the cinch. An English girth I could manage, with the straps and buckles that one tightens before and after getting into the saddle. But the cinch, which fastens with leather thongs which are threaded through a ring and knotted—that, on Sheba, was a complete misnomer. "Cinch" has come to mean a certainty—something secure and immoveable, deriving from this very type of girth-band. Cinch, applied to Sheba, however, meant it was a cinch the darned thing would slip, on account of her completely rotund stomach. Sherm said it would probably need tightening after a while and that had me worried for a start. One can tighten an English girth on the move, but a cinch is a different matter. So far as I could see I'd have to get off to do that. Get off? On the range? On a horse called

Sheba?

My first ride on her was when we went out on round-up on our second night at the ranch. Only a minor round-up—a matter of six miles or so down the valley to bring a bunch of heifers up past the ranch-house and turn them on to fresh grass. But a round-up all the same. Something I wouldn't have imagined in my wildest dreams. I never thought I'd be doing this when I battled outside the pub on Rory.

I can see the setting still. The log-built ranch house

with its barn and corral behind us, nestling in a sheltered scoop of the hills. The range rolling like the sea ahead of us, as far as the eye could see. Dark patches of trees on some of the hills, rocky outcrops on others . . . this had been Indian country. How often had Blackfoot scouts drawn rein up there, I wondered, watching what went on in the valley?

Now, as in a film, we rode through it ourselves, the evening sun casting long shadows over the grass. Sherm and his foreman, with coiled ropes on their saddles; Sherm's nephew, up from Wyoming on vacation. All of them wearing stetsons, riding long-stirruped in Western fashion. If Charles had had a stetson he'd have passed for a Westerner too, loping along as if he'd been born to it. This was the life, I thought to myself, as Sheba began to get up speed.

The ground though, it suddenly occurred to me, was pretty rough going for horses. Hummocks and hillocks and sudden hollows, and going downhill all the way. A gradual slope, admittedly, but with all those possible pitfalls—surely we ought not to be cantering? We were though. The horses, sure-footed as mountain goats, knew every inch of that range. We came to a creek with steep-sided banks that had dried up as a result of the hot weather. A small stream trickled through the middle of it, bordered by thick black mud. What did we do now? I wondered. Find a place to cross higher up? The horses wouldn't go through that.

Not English horses—or at any rate not without considerable urging. But Sheba was a Western horse. Straight down the bank she went, ploughing unhesitatingly through the mud, though it came up her sides as far as the stirrups. Up the other bank, into a canter as soon as she touched the top. She was in a hurry, she said. She had Business to attend to.

Attend to it she did. She had no help from me. All that uphill and down-dale had worked her saddle loose. I couldn't tighten it while I was on her. I didn't fancy getting off. And when I looked round for assistance, everybody else had gone. They were sweeping in wide circles towards distant groups of cattle that were scattered like confetti about the horizon; Charles with them, recognisable by the fact that he didn't have a hat on, yelling at me to come on.

I did that all right. Sheba had already picked out a group for herself and was heading for it at the double. All I could do was try to keep the saddle balanced and hope for rescue when we stopped. I did it by dint of, as I slipped over one way, standing up and pressing down hard on the other stirrup. A manoeuvre which became even more involved when we reached the group of cattle and Sheba started dodging about like a sheepdog. She darted to left and right, she feinted, she headed the heifers towards the others, whenever one tried to break away she was after it like a flash.... My contribution was that when we appeared likely to be going in a straight line for a few seconds I stood up and leaned as hard as I could to straighten the saddle—and, not wishing to incommode her, sat down hastily the moment she started to swerve.

I made it though. Eventually we had all the heifers together, the foreman locating the last few in a hollow on the other side of the hill. We had a breather for a few moments. Sherm tightened Sheba's cinch. Charles said he'd *wondered* what I'd been doing, dashing around standing up like that.

Eighty head of cattle we brought up the valley, their hurrying legs making a swishing sound, occasionally one of them bellowing in protest and another answering from the side. Five of us riding herd on them ... the shadows turning purple ... a deer leaping away from where it had been drinking at the stream. For me it was one of those moments one wishes would last for ever—except that Sheba's cinch had come loose again.

It was obviously her *pièce de resistance*. Fat-stomached she might be, but there was no doubt she also helped that saddle to come loose. Otherwise it could never have got where it did next morning, when we actually did very little more than walk.

Sherm, who was supervising the haymaking, had suggested we might like to ride on our own before breakfast. Why not go up to the head of the valley? he said. We could go up and circle the rim. Just watch out for bears as we went through the patch of trees on the top—though the horses would probably tell us if they were there.

That put the wind up me for a start. In theory, I knew, bears are harmless, so long as one doesn't antagonise them or get between a she-bear and her cub. It would be just my luck to do that by accident, though... and there was the little matter of Sheba's bit. The previous night she'd worn a curb, in case she got carried away with excitement. When she got worked up herding cattle, said Sherm, she could be a little difficult to stop. This morning, he said, he'd put her on a snaffle bit. On an ordinary ride it would be easier on her mouth. I'd have to watch her on it, though, he added. She and the roan were well-behaved, but when they got going they did tend not to want to stop.

That was all I needed. When we set out it was in single file with Charles very firmly in front. He was to stay there all the way, I said, in case she tried to take off. It was bad enough at home with Mio, but at least the Forest had a fence round it. If Sheba took off on rangeland I could see myself vanishing over the horizon for good.

To begin with, however, she had no intention of going anywhere. We went out through the corral gate, down the road, turning off to the right down a grassy gulley from the bottom of which a track led up over the shoulder of the hill. Halfway down the gulley Sheba, a look of innocence on her face, turned apparently aimlessly along a side-track that would have taken us back to the ranch. The roan turned equally innocently and followed after her. We had quite a job to get them round.

Even when we got them out of the gulley they kept looking back in the direction of the ranch. You could tell by their ears what they were thinking. Ought to be able to fool these greenhorns from England... what move should they try next? On up the hill we plodded. Gosh, it was hot, said Sheba. She'd *have* to stop for a rest. She looked down once more at the valley and headed for another little side-track she knew of. Go home now, should we? she asked. Before we met up with any bears?

In point of fact we didn't meet with any on that trip. They were eating raspberries in a neighbouring valley. But, my having insisted that we were going On, Sheba had a wow of a time putting the wind up me by pointing her ears suspiciously at every thicket... and even more so when she said she thought we'd better run this bit and get out of the danger area Faster.

Her cinch had come loose again. So loose this time that the saddle threatened to slip right round her stomach. Charles said he'd get off and tighten it, but I refused to consider that. In the middle of these trees? Where a bear might suddenly appear? And Sheba take off on a snaffle? I had a vision of Sheba and the roan in non-stop flight and Charles left behind with the bear. Which of us would be in the direst straits I wouldn't have liked to bet. I'd manage, I assured him, once more standing up.

It was, when I could spare the time to look at it, a wonderful morning. The sky a vivid, cloudless blue, the sun getting hotter every minute. On the furthest hills the blue-green patches of the pine forest had a hazy, slumbering look that added to the impression of coming heat. Beyond them rose the Rockies . . . jagged, violet, mystical as all far mountain ranges. On either side of the path the grass was knee-deep, studded with herbs and flowers. Gaillardias, sunflowers, Black-eyed Susans, the beautiful prairie rose. The tiny, small-leaved kinnikinnick, which the Indians used for tobacco. Low Saskatoon bushes, dripping with blue-black berries. The hum of insects was the only sound in the silence. A hawk hovered high overhead. Here again was the feeling of infinity which we had experienced on the Camargue. The endless sky, the boundless range, a very conscious sense of eternity. An awareness that we were but travellers on the river of time and that others had been here before us.

Indians and bears, according to Sheba, heading for another downward track she knew of, and this time we let her take it. It was now past nine o'clock. We hadn't quite reached the head of the valley, but we'd covered a good many miles. Breakfast was waiting, and Sheba's saddle was slipping and it would soon be too hot to ride. So we went down the path she selected for us. Steep... we had to take it carefully... but not so steep, so far as I could see, to warrant the fact that I had to clutch her mane to stop sliding over her head. Until I looked at her saddle and found she'd now got it up on her neck.

At the bottom, away from the risk of bears, Charles and I both got off. We had to, to heave the saddle back, and Charles tightened the cinch and hoisted me on again. We ambled back down the trail to breakfast as if we were proper cowhands, Charles leaning down, as if he'd done it all his life, to open the corral gate. We unsaddled the horses, patted them on their rumps, telling them that sure was some ride, and the two of them went over to their companions and started to munch on the scattered heaps of hay. Sheba seemed to be the centre of quite a gathering from which came a considerable number of snorts. It might have been that she was enjoying her breakfast. It could also have been that she was having a jolly good laugh.

Chapter Sixteen

Sheba wasn't the only one with bears on her mind. The next morning Charles and I got up at half-past five intending to ride before it got too hot but Sheba and the roan, keeping a watchful eye on us, were grazing high up on the hillside and refused to come down when they were called. We went for a walk instead and when we returned, around nine o'clock, we found Leonard anxiously scanning the landscape with binoculars. We'd been away so long, he said, he was sure we'd been chased by a bear. He was trying to spot us, up a tree, before setting out with a rescue party.

In fact we'd been visiting farther down the valley. Walking along the trail, after a constitutional round the hayfield, we'd met Sherm driving down it in the truck. The telephone had broken down and as he wanted the Vet he was just going down to call him from the neighbour's. He asked if we'd like to go with him. They bred Arab horses. He thought we might like to see them. We would, we said, but we were due back for breakfast. Oh, we wouldn't be long, said Sherm. It wasn't very far down the valley.

It was in fact ten miles. Ten miles to the nearest neighbour. With us at home it is three miles to the next *village*. We bumped down the dusty trail, over the interminable range, wondering why we'd ever considered our valley in England isolated. The ranch we eventually turned into is called the Lyndon place, though the name of its present owners is Lindsay. They welcomed us in and, over iced coffee in the ranch kitchen, told us its fascinating history.

Most appropriately, since it is now a horse-breeding ranch, it began with a horse. Some ninety years ago, when a Colonel Lyndon, the first settler in that part of Alberta, was looking for a place to build his homestead, he'd met an Indian who'd offered to show him a creek (a stream, that is) that would never run dry if the Colonel would give him the horse he was riding. It was a particularly fine pinto—a piebald we call them in England —and the Indians have always admired good horses, especially the showy "paints".

He probably hadn't expected to get it; the white men didn't always keep their word. But he'd brought the settler to this place, which was an ideal setting for a ranch. And here, at the spot where the spring gushes out of the rock, the Colonel had given him the horse. In addition he paid the Indians cash for the land— something that was practically unheard of. As a result, after he'd built the ranch-house, when he returned, as he sometimes did, to England, the Blackfoot Indians moved in and pitched their camp around it, constituting themselves its guard. He could go away for months at a time. When he came back, everything was just as he had left it. Other settlers might find one of their horses missing, or a steer killed and carried off for food. Never on the Lyndon ranch. It was absolutely inviolable. And the Indian, in turn, had kept faith about the spring. In ninety years it has never once run dry.

It is all there still. The clearing around the ranch-house where the Blackfoot teepees once stood; the spring-house, built of logs, over the source of the spring. It is cold inside, like a cave, with the icy stream gushing through it and stepping-stones across the floor. The Lyndons kept their milk and meat and butter in the spring-house and there is the place where the buckets were filled. Here, where we were standing, not so very long ago stood an Indian and a settler with a horse ... In the West the past is never very far away. At times like this one can almost reach out and touch it.

In the corral was a sight the Colonel and the Indian would both have appreciated—a batch of Arab brood mares and their foals. With them, importantly—very like Sheba in colouring and looks, except that he wasn't fat—was Jared, the Lindsays' prize stallion. The ranch living-room was hung with ribbons the horses had won at shows that year and the twenty-foot-long stone hearth was banked with trophies. Statuettes, rose-bowls, great silver cups—many of them won by Jared. Most of them in normal events but some in the Arab parade classes which are so popular in North America, in which the horses are themselves dressed up in trappings that out-Orient the Orient. They wear golden saddle cloths, crupper cloths, head-caps, bridles dripping with tassels and imitation jewels. They showed us Jared's, and the outfit worn by his rider ... a golden sheik's costume, with an Indian rajah's turban and gold, bejewelled slippers. Jared liked dressing up, they said. I'll bet he did. No wonder he looked so important. All those wives, and these trappings for state occasions. I bet Mio would have fancied himself, too, in that saddle cloth and a turban.

The horse is still the king in the West and there are

harness shops and riding outfitters in every town. The one thing missing, unlike the Camargue, is that one no longer sees hitching posts. In these days of four-line highways the rancher goes to town by truck or car, leaving his horses at home except for shows or rodeos. The rodeo, of course, is the Westerners' favourite sport. According to the chroniclers the first one was held just after the Civil War, the outcome of the cowboys' off-duty pastime of seeing who could stay longest on an unbroken horse. One rodeo event, however—the bull-riding— goes much farther back than

that. Practised in Western arenas as it was two thousand years ago in Crete, undoubtedly it derives from the same mystical source as the bull-play of the Camargue.

Many of the modern rodeos are big, commercial affairs, put on in stadiums in large towns. We were fortunate to see one in its original form, held on an Alberta ranch, and we went to it as the result of a stranger arriving at the SN ranch one day driving a large car with a horse-box in tow. He wore a checked shirt, a Stetson, jeans and dusty riding boots and Sherm introduced him as a friend of his, Doc West, just up from Cheyenne, in Wyoming, where he'd been taking part in the roping events at the rodeo. He'd been a wizard with the rope in his younger days, apparently, and was pretty good at it still. He must have been, to have competed at Cheyenne. He wasn't as fast as he had been, he said—roping is a young man's game—but he didn't do it for the prize money. He really *was* a doctor, roping was his hobby, and he was in fact on holiday. Doing a tour of the rodeos—he was on his way north to another one—and staying at the SN for the night.

As he unloaded his horse—a light chestnut, almost a palomino—he told us something about roping and the importance of the horse in the game. Roping originated with the custom, on the old, unfenced open range, of rounding up the calves every year and branding them, so that it would be known to whom they belonged. For this the cowboy had to isolate a calf from the herd, rope it while it was running, bring it down, dismount and tie its legs ready for branding—speed being the essence of the operation and co-operation from the horse essential.

This has now become a rodeo event, with a prize for the fastest time . . . thirteen seconds, maybe less, from the time the calf comes out of the pen. The horse—nowadays often a quarter-horse, so-called because of his dynamic speed over a quarter of a mile—tears after the calf, puts its rider in his favourite position for roping, brakes a split second after the loop drops over the calf's neck, while his rider is dismounting at a run. And then —the most incredible part of the whole manoeuvre— entirely on his own, without a rider on his back; with the rope, attached to his saddle horn, completely out of human control—the horse plays the calf like a trout. Watching it carefully, backing or going sideways when necessary, keeping the rope taut so that the calf is unable to get up. Only when his human partner has reached the calf, tied its legs and held his hands up, does a roping horse relax.

This, we said, we must see for ourselves, and Doc West, who knew the whole calendar of rodeos, said there was one that weekend at Cowley, about forty miles away. He wouldn't be at it—he was heading farther north—but it was the nearest one for us to go to.

So we went to the Cowley rodeo and the setting was perfect. Exactly as the first rodeo might have been. The wooden-barred enclosure in the vast expanse of rangeland, the Rockies, as ever, on the horizon. People greeting each other. Stetsons and bright-coloured shirts and bandanas. The whinny of excited horses. The chink of spurs and harness, the dusty ring and the hot sun shining down on it all. And then a trumpet fanfare and the flags being ridden in; part of the rodeo ceremonial. The Canadian flag with its maple leaf, the Stars and Stripes for America, carried in by two riders and cantered round the ring. The flags, then, brought to the centre. The audience standing, singing O! Canada. Once more I found myself wondering whether this was real.

It was real all right. In no time at all the chute door was up and the first bareback rider was in the ring. We were watching, not from a grandstand in a city arena, but from a wooden bench just over a fencing rail. We could hear the horse's breathing. We were powdered by the dust he threw up. We could see every movement of the rider's muscles ... arching himself tautly as the horse's head went down, bracing himself to stay with him when he jumped. The bareback competitor's only aid is a handgrip like the handle of a suitcase, fastened to a leather strap that circles the horse's stomach. He has to ride one-handed—he is disqualified if he touches either the horse or himself with the other—and he must spur the horse's shoulders all the way. The spurs are blunt, and the rowels must not be locked, so that they cannot rake or damage the horse. They simply make him buck as if he were fitted with springs instead of legs, and this goes on for eight pitching, thumping seconds.

At the end of that time a horn blows and, if the competitor is still on the horse, a couple of pickup men ride in to get him off. One gallops alongside the bucking horse and ropes it; the competitor leans sideways, grabs the pickup man's shoulders and leaps around his back and to the ground; the second pickup man deals with the now riderless horse, leading it off towards the exit.

Another class, with much the same rules as for bareback riding, is the Saddle Bronc event. In this, as is obvious from the name, the horses are saddled, but it doesn't make riding them any easier. They are usually bigger and, if possible, even more spirited than the barebacks, and like erupting volcanoes to sit. Losing a stirrup disqualifies the rider in this event as surely as being bucked off, while the one-sided rein, attached only to a plain halter, may assist the rider's balance at one moment and have him over the horse's head the next. A good many rodeo riders end the season on crutches, but next year they will be back for more.

And the other rodeo classes—steer-wrestling and bull-riding—don't exactly qualify as soothing sports.

In steer-wrestling the competitor, known as the dogger, gallops after a steer which has been released from a chute, falls sideways from his horse on to the steer's back as he passes it, seizes the animal's handlebar-like horns and, with an agile twist that brings him in front of it, attempts to wrestle it to the ground. He has a mounted companion, called a hazer, whose job it is to keep the steer running when it comes out of the chute. The hazer is of little help if the dogger gets into difficulties; a competitor can lose his life at this game, on the end of those carving-knife horns. The most dangerous event of all, though, is without any doubt the bull-riding.

A steer is not normally bent on murder, though it may do damage with its horns. The huge Brahma bulls used in the bull-riding events, however, are definitely out to kill. The clown, funny though he may be, who tumbles about the ring during the bull-riding, has another purpose beyond amusing the spectators.

Brave, quick-witted, a clever contortionist—it is his job to distract the bull's attention when its rider is thrown off. No pickup men are allowed in the arena during bull-riding because of the danger of the horses being gored. Only the clown can save a rider in an emergency, and in doing so may be himself caught by the horns.

The rider straddles the bull bareback, holding, one-handed, a rope that circles its tremendous girth. He must stay on for eight seconds to qualify, and is very often thrown as soon as he hurtles out of the chute. The bulls buck like the toughest of broncos, with the added hazard of being able to rake their sides with their horns. One doesn't feel sorry for these giants as one does for the little bulls of the Camargue. These can shake a man from their backs like a horse twitching off a fly, and their jack-knifing eight seconds in the arena are over in a flash. They are not nervous of the spectators. They are obviously in splendid condition. For all that, steer-wrestling and bull-riding are not my cup of tea. I went to see the horses.

A rodeo finishes traditionally with a barrel-race, the only event in which women riders take part. It involves riding at top speed, clockwise and counter-clockwise, round three barrels—usually oil-drums—set in the form of a clover-leaf. It may not sound very exciting after the other events, but the audience loves it. The competitors wear sumptuous outfits, usually of gold or silver lamé—with, of course, the ubiquitous stetson on top; their horses are magnificent; and my goodness, can those Western girls ride! The horses go round the barrels like greyhounds, often at an angle at which the rider's inside foot is almost touching the ground. There can be a considerable amount of luck in the other rodeo events, but in the barrel race the criterion is skill.

After that comes the prize-giving and the picnic teas on the grass, and wandering around looking at the horses while a cowboy band plays in the background. And if anyone is wondering how Charles and I managed to go to a rodeo without leaving our individual mark on it, they may be interested to know that it was at this point that we did.

Strolling around, taking in the atmosphere, we came across a couple of girl riders trying to turn on a tap. It was a standpipe with a hose attached to it, it had been turned off very tightly, and they just couldn't get it to work. Charles turned it on, I held the hose and filled their buckets for them—and then we couldn't turn it off again. Like many ranch water supplies it was fed from a powerful spring, and it was shooting out of that hosepipe as if we'd fractured a water-main. When the others, wondering where we'd got to, came to look for us—though as Leonard said, they knew it couldn't be a bear this time—they found us soaked to the skin, with several very wet Westerners around us, looking as if we were playing at Keystone Cops.

Combined effort eventually turned the tap off. Several people asked if we were from England. At least it proved we could hold our end up, even at a Western rodeo.

Chapter Seventeen

The rodeo was only one of the highlights of our trip, but this is a book about horses. Our other adventures in Canada must wait for another occasion. I should perhaps mention the bears though, since Leonard was always expecting us to meet up with one and, in the fullness of time, we did.

When it happened we were guests on another ranch, in a valley which ran parallel with Sherm's. Its owner, known to all her friends as Babe, was a character after our own hearts. She was—other people told us, this, not Babe—one of the finest horsewomen in Alberta. Her father had been one of the earliest pioneers in the Waterton area of the Rockies. She had countless stories about him and hundreds of photographs he had taken ... but that, again, must wait for another time. For the moment it is enough that we went looking for raspberries one morning on the hillside behind her ranch-house. Two days earlier Babe had picked a bucketful up there herself and we thought they'd be nice for lunch. We wondered why we found scarcely a cupful ourselves. Perhaps they were over, I said. And then, as we wandered higher up the hill, Charles suddenly froze and gripped my arm.

"Straight up in front of you," he muttered. About two hundred yards above us, half-lying under a stunted cypress but with its head and ears raised in our direction, was a big black Canadian bear. Obviously that was who had eaten the raspberries. Bears are very fond of fruit.

Other than knowing about not getting between a female and its cub I hadn't a clue what to do. Climb a tree in an emergency, of course, but that seemed overdoing it a bit at this stage... this one was still half asleep and they were said not to be deliberately aggressive. There were, too, a lot of trees between us and the ranch. If we went up the nearest one, which we would if we were going to do it at all, there would be a solid screen of foliage between us and Leonard's binoculars. We could be up it, unspotted, for hours.

So we turned round and strolled unhurriedly back down to the valley—not, it must be admitted, without one or two glances to the rear to see if we were being followed—and in that... Charles having remembered the instructions from his youth... apparently we did the right thing. "Never run from a bear," Babe told us later. "They may look clumsy when they're running themselves, with their back legs ahead of their ears—but they can travel downhill faster than a horse, and nearly as fast on the flat."

She gave us several other tips about them. That one can tell when a bear is near, for instance, by a smell like that of a wet dog—and, paradoxically, that we mustn't take the dogs out with us now that we knew there was a bear about. Far from acting as a protection, bears hate dogs and will often deliberately attack them where they would run away from humans.

It *was* a bear, too. Not, as someone suggested, a log. Next morning the ranch foreman found its tracks around the corral. In the old days, as with coyotes, he would have gone for his gun—there was a pedigree cow and her calf in one of the enclosures. All that happened in these more enlightened times, however, was that that night the cow and calf were moved into the barn for safety and the corral light left on. The bear wouldn't attack the cow, said Babe. But it might, just as a long-shot, have its eye on the day-old calf.

In point of fact it didn't. All that bear was interested in, having harvested the raspberries, was the patch of saskatoons on the opposite hill. There she was next morning, clearly visible through the ranch window as we sat at breakfast, stripping the berries from the saskatoon bushes with a massive black steel-hooked claw, while a cub, obviously warned as to what she'd do to *him* if he dared set foot in the open, appeared and disappeared like a conjurer's rabbit in a larger bush at her side.

They were there for several mornings. When, a few days later we drove in the ranch jeep over a Texas gate (a cattle grid to us in England; Texas was obviously where it originated) and yet another bear, disturbed by the rattling, reared up on its haunches to look at us from the undergrowth by the roadside as we passed—when that happened we thought we must just about be qualifying as bear spotters of the year. Then we went on to the Rockies proper and found we hadn't seen anything yet.

There they have the eight-foot grizzlies, as well as the black bears of the foothills, and the talks given by the staff naturalists in the national parks always begin with a caution about bears. "If you should meet up with one," said the lecturer the night we were in the audience at Waterton, "your first reaction will probably

be to wonder whether it is a black bear or a grizzly. Your second may be to climb the nearest tree. This in fact should answer your query. If it's a black bear it can climb and come up after you. If it's a grizzly it can't climb, so it will pull the tree down." Hearty laughter, as the lecturer intended. Bears normally run away from human beings. A few weeks previously, however, that was as far as the lecturer got. At that point a black bear ambled into the open-air auditorium and the audience vanished from its rough-hewn log seats like snow before an Albertan chinook.

Some people looked for bears. Others studiously avoided them. Climbing the trail to Bertha Lake one day we heard what sounded like cowbells ahead of us—and round the next corner came a hiking party whose leader wore an overhead framework attached to his rucksack, from which hung so many bells he clanked like a herd of Simmenthals.

It must have driven his companions crazy, but it certainly kept off the bears. Neither we nor the hikers saw any on the trail that day, though there was no doubt they were around. That night a girl taking a shower in one of the lakeside cabins heard the outer door handle rattling. Her parents had gone out to buy groceries. Thinking they had forgotten the key, she wrapped herself in a towel, opened the door—and looked straight into the face of a bear.

She slammed the door, rushed into the bathroom, opened the window and screamed. Other tourists, running to the rescue, saw the bear streaking across the camp-ground in the direction of the Bertha trail and next morning there was quite a run on bear bells.

We ourselves were staying at a motor lodge at the more populated end of the lake. Discussing the incident in the hotel lounge that night I said "Imagine them

coming as close as that!"

"You think that's close?" said the proprietor, and took us out to the hotel kitchen. There, preserved as a memento of a bear's visit to the Kilmorey, was a five-clawed gouge down the kitchen door and several pieces missing from its framework. The bear, which had somehow managed to shut itself in, had also climbed on to the draining board and taken a claustrophobic swipe at the ceiling.

No, nobody had been hurt, said the hotel owner. The bear had only been looking for food. Eventually someone had opened the door from the outside with a broom handle and it had ambled off up the road back to its mountains. In any case that had been ages ago. It wasn't a normal occurrence.

Maybe not, but that night I checked the doorbolts myself. I didn't want anyone eating my porridge.

That was almost the end of our Canadian trip. Shortly after that we returned to England. Even as the plane took off from Edmonton, however, we knew that we would go back. To the mountains we'd grown to love, the people who'd become our friends, the animals we'd met—and those we hadn't. We hadn't seen a grizzly yet, I reminded Charles . . . and the tales we'd heard about the wolves were absolutely fascinating. The valley would seem a bit tame now, wouldn't it? I said. What made me think that? asked Charles.

He was right. Within an hour of getting home Father Adams was leaning on our front gate, catching us up with the news. Who'd got married. Who ought to be. Miss Wellington had bought a parrot. Din' half swear, said Father Adams; we ought to go up and hear him. 'N' she from the Tower House 'n' old Sam Ferry had got to be proper cronies. . . . "They've *what*?" I said incredulously, thinking of the woman from the Tower House as I knew her, with her ideas of position and grandeur.

It seemed she'd been riding through the village one day—one one horse as usual, busily leading the other—and just as she passed Sam Ferry's cottage a bucketful of water shot out through the gateway, frightening them and making them rear. Behind the water came Sam, swishing it furiously with a broom.

"What do you think you're doing?" she asked. "Washing down me path," he replied. He paused, and fixed her with an uncompromising blue eye. "People bin usin' it as a w.c.," he said.

It was one of his perennial complaints—that late homegoers from the pub used his alleyway to nip into if they'd forgotten about doing it before. "Ought to be a Convenience on the village green," he was always protesting. "The Council ought to do something about it."

Not only had the woman from the Tower House rallied to his cause . . . at last she had something her husband could really go into... but when she'd heard about Sam's ancestry... that his forefathers had been there since before the Armada... "Up on this hill was where we lit the bonfire," I could imagine Sam telling her, as, when he got the chance, he told everybody... she'd been so impressed with his pedigree, even though it didn't contain any earls, that she'd come down off her high horse with a bang and they chatted at his gate nearly every day. She no longer led a spare horse. Sam's grand-daughter, Norma, could ride. As usual the village had broken down the barriers. The processes of democracy were under way.

We brought Annabel back from the farm. We fetched the cats back from Low Knap. They didn't appear to have missed us one bit. Shebalu had pollarded the willow in their run by way of a holiday task, said Mrs. Francis, but it would probably recover in time. Seeley had been his usual lovable self. They were a gorgeous pair, she said.

We drove home with them, let them out of their basket, accompanied them up on to the hillside. It was still the adder season and Seeley had once been bitten by one up there. Usually I went up with them on guard alone, but this time Charles came with me. We sat in the evening sunshine, talking over our trip, the cats busily prospecting on the hillside behind us. Very like Canada, wasn't it? said Charles, looking around at the Forest. Out there, though, we wouldn't be able to have the cats near the woods like this... there could easily be a bear in those very trees.... At which moment Seeley, who'd just made a pounce in the grass near a gorse bush, leapt several feet in the air.

"Quick!" I shouted. "An adder!" said Charles,

rushing to pick Seeley up. He missed him by a hairsbreadth and, to my amazement, started spluttering like mad. "Catch him!" he said. "He's foaming at the mouth! He spat some of it into mine and it's horrible!" And sure enough Seeley was charging around the hillside scattering foam in all directions.

I got him, rushed him indoors, with Shebalu following after me, and he continued foaming under the table. I was frantically looking up the vet's telephone number when Charles came in and announced that the cause was a toad. He'd found it in the grass, right where

Seeley'd pounced, when he checked to see if there was an adder. We'd read about this somewhere—that toads, when attacked by animals, can spurt an offensive liquid out of their warts in self-defence. It had never happened to us before, though, in all our years of cat-keeping. Was it poisonous? was the next thought that flashed through our minds. So there we were, within hours of coming back from Canada, hunting feverishly through the reference books. It was all right. The liquid was harmless. But what had I said about life in the Valley being tame?

A few days later I went up to the stables, my thoughts running along the same lines. The boundless range, the

Rockies, riding on round-up on Sheba... how unexciting riding in the Forest would seem after that. Mrs. Hutchings put my musing into words. Riding Mio would be child's play to me now, she said. Was I sure I wouldn't like Jasper—perhaps after a breakfast of oats?

I laughed. She was only joking. And there was no horse in the world like Mio. I hugged his neck, asked him how he'd been, climbed up on his sleek dun back. We'd had our ride and were on our way home when it happened. While I'd been away the Hutchings had bought a horse called Alexander. Powerful, strong, very eager—he'd been ridden with the Beaufort Hunt. Coming back down the track from the gate which led to the Downs, Alexander, full of himself, started to go. His rider couldn't hold him, and then Mio took off as well.

He hadn't half missed me, he snorted, as we zoomed familiarly down the track. That horse Alexander was getting above himself. Now we'd show him what galloping meant!

No we wouldn't, I said, sitting down and reining him firmly. *He* didn't have a slipping saddle. I'd got some experience while I was in Canada. He could stop right here and *behave*.

I wondered why the reins had no effect—until I noticed they were both on the same side of his head. Rearing, prancing, tossing his head about, he'd got the left one over his right ear. I lost a stirrup. My leg went up in the air. We thundered on down the track. Here was where I came off at last, I thought. Which was the softest spot to fall?

I must have learned something from riding Sheba.

Nobody was more surprised than I was when I recovered myself, turned him in a circle and stopped. She thought I was off that time, said Mrs. Hutchings as she caught me up. By golly, so did I, I gasped.

Well, it looked as if things were back to normal, said Mrs. Hutchings as the cavalcade rode home.

WITHDRAWN
No longer the property of the
Boston Public Library.
Sale of this material benefits the Library

Boston Public Library

Copley Square

GENERAL LIBRARY

PR6039
.O75M3
1974AX

2636630342

The Date Due Card in the pocket indicates the date on or before which this book should be returned to the Library. Please do not remove cards from this pocket.